D0283683

DESIGNED FOR LOVE

Acclaim for Erin Dutton's Fiction

Sequestered Hearts

"*Sequestered Hearts* by first time novelist, Erin Dutton, is everything a romance should be. It is teeming with longing, heartbreak, and of course, love. I have reread this book twice, and as pure romances go, it is one of the best in print today… *Sequestered Hearts* is packed with raw emotion, but filled with tender moments too. The author writes with sophistication that one would expect from a veteran author…Dutton's words match perfectly with the emotion she has created. Every encounter oozes with Ben's and Cori's hunger for each other. *Sequestered Hearts* is one book that cannot be overlooked. It is romance at its finest." —*Just About Write*

"*Sequestered Hearts* tells of two very private women dealing with the magnetic attraction between them. It is the story of the difficult dance between them, and how each is able to resolve her individual issues and find happiness. Cori and Bennett are likeable, well developed characters and their story will keep the reader turning the pages to see how it all works out." —*Just About Write*

Fully Involved

"Set in Nashville, *Fully Involved* starts with a bang as fire engines race toward a fire at the downtown Hilton Hotel… Dutton literally fills the pages with smoke as she vividly describes the scene. She is equally skilled at showing her readers Reid's feelings of guilt and rage…*Fully Involved* explores the emotional depths of…two very different women. Each woman struggles with loss, change, and the magnetic attraction they have for each other. Their relationship sizzles, flames, and ignites with a page turning intensity. This is an exciting read about two very intriguing women." *—Just About Write*

"Back when Isabel Grant was the tag-along little sister who annoyed them, tomboy Reid Webb and boyhood pal Jimmy Grant considered the girl an intrusion…Years later, Isabel… comes back into Reid's life…and childhood frictions—complicated by Reid's guilty attraction to Isabel—flare into emotional warfare. This being a lesbian romance, no plot points are spoiled by the fact that Reid and Isabel, both stubborn to the core, end up in each other's arms. But Dutton's studied evocation of the macho world of firefighting gives the formulaic story extra oomph—and happily ever after is what a good romance is all about, right?" *—Q Syndicate*

By the Author

Sequestered Hearts

Fully Involved

A Place to Rest

Designed for Love

Visit us at www.boldstrokesbooks.com

DESIGNED FOR LOVE

by

Erin Dutton

2008

DESIGNED FOR LOVE

© 2008 By Erin Dutton. All Rights Reserved.

ISBN 10: 1-60282-038-4
ISBN 13: 978-1-60282-038-8

This Trade Paperback Original Is Published By
Bold Strokes Books, Inc.
P.O. Box 249
Valley Falls, NY 12185

First Edition: November 2008

THIS IS A WORK OF FICTION. NAMES, CHARACTERS, PLACES, AND INCIDENTS ARE THE PRODUCT OF THE AUTHOR'S IMAGINATION OR ARE USED FICTITIOUSLY. ANY RESEMBLANCE TO ACTUAL PERSONS, LIVING OR DEAD, BUSINESS ESTABLISHMENTS, EVENTS, OR LOCALES IS ENTIRELY COINCIDENTAL.

THIS BOOK, OR PARTS THEREOF, MAY NOT BE REPRODUCED IN ANY FORM WITHOUT PERMISSION.

Credits
Editor: Shelley Thrasher
Production Design: Stacia Seaman
Cover Design By Sheri (graphicartist2020@hotmail.com)

Acknowledgments

As always, thanks to Radclyffe for your leadership and for each opportunity to tell a new story. Shelley Thrasher, I never thought I could describe the editorial process as painless, but with you, on this project, it was pretty darn close.

In this, my fourth book, I want to thank Toni, Dana, and Jeanne—for always being willing to talk out story lines, read whatever I ask them to, and offer honest opinions.

Dedication

To Gertrude,

because there wouldn't be a George without you.

CHAPTER ONE

Jillian Sealy climbed out of her BMW, tugging at her short skirt as it rode up her thigh. She flipped her sunglasses onto her head and dubiously studied the establishment in front of her. The building had definitely seen better days. Avocado green paint had long ago started peeling off the wood siding, and from the grime on the windows, she guessed it had been years since they were washed. The sign above the door read Johnson & Son Construction.

After only two days in Redmond, a small town in east Tennessee, she could almost picture the beefy rednecks who worked inside. She pulled on the hem of her skirt again and glanced down at her white silk blouse and black Tahari jacket to ensure she wasn't revealing too much cleavage. She wasn't in the mood to compete with her breasts for the men's attention.

"Well, let's get this over with," she muttered. As she crossed the gravel lot she cursed the thin layer of dust that settled on her Jimmy Choo sling backs.

When she stepped inside the front door the occupants didn't disappoint her. Three men in jeans and flannel shirts looked her way, and she could practically feel their gaze drop down her body.

"May I help you, ma'am?" The bravest of them took off his ball cap and stepped forward. At least he had manners.

"I'm looking for Mr. Johnson."

A bald man wearing a chambray shirt with *Johnson & Son* embroidered on the left pocket entered through a door at the right and said, "Well, you've found him."

"I'm Jillian Sealy. We spoke on the phone."

"Yes, Miss Sealy, come into the office." He indicated the door he still stood in front of and waited while she entered ahead of him.

"As I told you on the phone, Mr. Johnson, I've recently inherited Mary Connor's house. I intend to fix it up and sell it, and I'll need a contractor." She'd been surprised to learn that her great-aunt had left her the house. But it had offered the perfect reason to get out of Cincinnati. She'd barely hesitated before packing up and driving south.

"Please, call me Bud. My sympathies on your loss, ma'am. I did plenty of work for Mrs. Connor over the years. If you hire us, I'll send my kid's crew. They're my best."

She'd found the listing for Mr. Johnson's company in Aunt Mary's address book. Now that she'd met him, she was even more confident she'd made the right call. Bud Johnson struck her as an honest, hardworking man.

Thirty minutes later, after she'd finished outlining her plans for the house, Bud gave her a good-faith estimate.

"I think we've got a deal, then," she said, extending her hand, and he shook it firmly.

"Good. I'll send Wil over when it's convenient for you so you can review your plans."

❖

The next morning Jillian sat in the front-porch swing making notes on her plans for the house. It was turning into a pleasant day, warm with just enough of a breeze to ruffle the leaves of the large sycamore. She made a note to have a tree service prune the sprawling branches so the house would be more visible from the street.

"Miss Sealy?"

Jillian looked up and her breath caught in her throat. The powerfully built woman standing at the bottom of the steps regarded her with eyes the color of light sapphires. Her black hair swept back from her face in thick waves and barely brushed the collar of her denim jacket. Her white T-shirt was tucked into jeans so well worn the denim looked as soft as flannel. Deeply tanned skin stretched over wide cheekbones.

Jillian realized the woman was still waiting for her to speak. "Yes?"

"I'm Wil. You met with my father yesterday. He told me you were expecting me." Jillian sensed a raw edge in Wil, yet the sensuous alto with a lilting accent seemed oddly gentle.

"Yes." She recovered a bit of her composure. "Yes. I'm sorry. It's Johnson and Son—I guess I was thrown."

"Actually, the original 'Johnson' was my grandfather. My father didn't have any sons, but when he took over he didn't want to change the name." Wil shoved her hands in her pocket and the motion tugged her jeans lower, accentuating her narrow hips.

"I'm sorry, I'm being rude. Can I get you anything to drink?" Jillian forced her eyes to Wil's face.

"No, ma'am."

Jillian laughed. "Lord, save me from Southern hospitality. Please don't call me ma'am."

"Yes, Miss Sealy."

"It's Jillian."

Wil smiled, revealing a small gap between otherwise perfect teeth. "Okay. Jillian."

"Let's get started, then," Jillian said, more abruptly than she'd intended. The gentle way Wil's low voice caressed her name was distracting and she needed to get back on track. "Would you like a tour while I explain what I have in mind?"

"Sure."

"Well, for starters, I plan to do some of the smaller projects myself, like replacing the boards on this porch and giving it a fresh coat of paint. So I'll just need you to handle the larger issues while I'm working on those." She had decided on projects she could do herself so she could spend more money on the quality touches that would maximize her profit when she sold.

"That's fine. So we'll just do what you need us to and then you can finish up your tasks."

"Actually, I'd planned on doing the work simultaneously."

"What's your hurry?"

"If we finish quickly I can get it on the market sooner."

"My crew isn't used to working with the homeowner underfoot."

"Well, then I'll try not to be *underfoot*." Jillian's tone purposely indicated that there would be no argument. "Let's start in the dining room."

Aware that she'd just been put in her place, Wil climbed the steps to the front porch that spanned the width of the house. The exterior needed paint, but the buttery yellow shade wouldn't be Wil's first choice.

After automatically assessing the outside of the house, Wil turned her attention to her new client. She couldn't see Jillian's eyes behind her sunglasses, but finely arched brows had lifted in surprise as she'd first looked at Wil. She couldn't even guess how much Jillian spent on products to make her skin look so soft and flawless. Wil didn't see any of the lines that marred her own face.

She glanced at the waistband of Jillian's jeans where her neatly pressed button-down shirt was tucked in, revealing the expected designer label. As her gaze drifted farther down, she wondered if it was the expensive jeans that made Jillian's ass appear so perfect. In just minutes, she'd pegged Jillian as high-maintenance and, though incredibly attractive, probably far too uptight for Wil's liking.

They entered the house and passed through the foyer into the dining room. Wil noted the pocket doors set in the ornately carved woodwork. She tested one, satisfied to feel it glide out smoothly.

"In here, there's just that bit of molding that needs to be fixed."

"That shouldn't be a big deal."

Jillian stepped into the kitchen and turned, causing Wil to stop quickly. At least six inches shorter, Jillian tilted her head back to meet Wil's eyes. "I also need to have the wiring inspected in the entire house. Can you recommend an electrician?"

"We've got a guy we usually use. I can give him a call or I can get you his number." Jillian had removed her sunglasses and Wil could now see that her irises were green, with flecks of gold. Realizing that she was staring into Jillian's eyes, Wil dropped her gaze. But that was a mistake as well, since the three buttons open on Jillian's shirt revealed the curve of her breasts. Wil's stomach clenched and she curled her fingers into her palms to quell the sudden urge to trace them inside the edge of Jillian's shirt.

"If you don't mind, I'll leave that up to you. In here, I want to push that far wall out a bit to open up the space and put in an island." Jillian pivoted away and swept a hand past the wall in question and then indicated the one next to it. Wil fought to keep her breathing even and was astonished at how unaffected Jillian seemed by a moment that had rocked her. "Here I want to put in a bay window and make a breakfast nook. We'll add recessed lighting and all new cabinets and countertops, to go with the updated appliances I plan to buy."

"You're going to spend most of your money in here," Wil commented, trying to focus on the details. She pulled a small notebook from her jacket pocket and jotted notes as Jillian spoke.

"Kitchens sell houses," Jillian responded quickly.

"You sound like a realtor."

"I am."

"Really? Local?" Wil was certain she would have run into Jillian before now if she was local. They'd worked with most of the area realtors at one time or another. She guessed Jillian had five or six years on her, putting her in her mid-thirties. Maybe she'd started a second career.

"Cincinnati, but I'll be here until I sell this house."

"If you want things done in a hurry, it's going to be difficult for you to be living here at the same time."

"Well, the kitchen won't be a problem since I don't do a lot of cooking anyway." Jillian waved off her concern and headed for the living room. "I'll set myself up in one of the spare rooms since it only needs fresh paint."

The living room boasted high ceilings with crown molding and large double-hung windows. Wil really did love these old houses. She could tell from Jillian's attention to detail that she had put a lot of thought into this restoration.

As Jillian led her through the rest of the house, she was overly aware of Wil's scent, like sandalwood and summer rain. She couldn't suppress her reaction, but hoped she hid it well. Wil occasionally asked questions, and Jillian was surprised by how well she already seemed to understand her vision for the house.

In the master bathroom, Jillian said, "Next to the kitchen, I think most of the work will be in here. I want to add a tiled shower stall in the corner, a claw-foot tub, and a new pedestal sink."

Jillian kept her tone controlled despite the fact that they stood very close in the small room. While Wil continued to jot notes, Jillian stared at her mouth and wondered how it would feel to kiss her, to trace Wil's thin lips with the tip of her tongue before plunging inside. Would Wil respond with the energy Jillian felt vibrating within her?

When Wil drew her bottom lip between her teeth in concentration, Jillian imagined gently sucking it. She jerked her eyes away, but failed to dispel the image.

"Right, so that's the tour." Jillian moved past Wil, carefully avoiding contact. She'd never spent so much time fantasizing about someone she'd just met, and she didn't think touching Wil, even accidentally, would help her condition. She led Wil back to the living room. In an effort to fill the uncomfortable silence, she kept talking. "Aunt Mary left me the furnishings too. I'll put most of them in storage while the work is being done. Then, I don't know, maybe an auction. There are actually some nice pieces here."

Wil nodded. "I'm sorry for your loss. Were you close?"

"Not at all. I was here briefly five years ago when her husband died. I don't know why she left me the house. Except that she didn't have any children of her own."

"Perhaps she felt a connection with you."

"I rarely saw her," Jillian said. It was impossible to feel connected to someone you barely knew. Wasn't it? Yet here she was feeling as if she would go to bed with this stranger without a second's hesitation. Shaking her head, she dismissed the idea. "Given my profession, it's more likely she knew I would be best equipped to sell the house."

For a moment Wil looked like she might argue, but instead she headed for the front door.

"My crew is finishing up another job today. You and I should go to the hardware store and order the cabinets and some fixtures. I'll get a tentative schedule drawn up so you'll know when you'll have room to work on your projects. Is it okay if I bring that by tomorrow?"

"I'll look forward to seeing you then."

Jillian watched from the porch as Wil walked toward the white Chevy pickup bearing the Johnson & Son logo. When Wil turned around to glance at her before climbing in the truck, Jillian flushed, hoping Wil was too far away to tell that she'd been transfixed by her confident swagger.

❖

Jillian walked out the front door and looked around, marveling at her surroundings. For the time being, she'd landed in Small Town, U.S.A. Aunt Mary's house was just four tree-lined blocks from the Redmond town square, complete with a drugstore, city hall, hardware store, and a diner, Jillian's lunch destination. She hadn't been kidding when she told Wil she didn't cook, and since she'd arrived only days before, she hadn't taken time to get even the barest essentials. Wil and her crew would probably be tearing up the kitchen by next week, so Jillian figured there was no reason to stock up when she could take a short walk for some country home cooking.

It was an idyllic early summer day, almost too much so. Sunlight slashed through gaps in the full shade trees overhead, and birds chirped cheerfully. The Mayberry atmosphere in this town felt surreal in comparison to the constant hum of the city Jillian was used to hearing outside the window of her downtown condo, and she'd been having trouble sleeping.

When she'd first driven into town she'd worried she wouldn't survive for the couple of months it would take to fix up the house. After all, there wasn't a Starbucks for miles. And she doubted she'd be able to get a massage or a decent facial at the one salon in town. From a quick look through the window as she walked past, she could tell nothing had changed inside in close to a decade. The only surprise so far had been the sign in the window at the diner announcing the presence of Wi-Fi.

Everything she'd encountered here felt out of place, including the intensity of her initial attraction to Wil Johnson. To put it bluntly, blue-collar wasn't normally her type. She tended to go for polished and professional. Usually, she dated women that she had things in common with, but it was getting harder and harder to find someone who didn't quickly bore her. After all, you could have only so much intelligent conversation. She got that with her friends. What she wanted was a grand passion. Her reaction to women was often mostly intellectual and practical, nothing like the visceral response to Wil's physicality. She couldn't deny the spread of hot arousal when she'd found herself the subject of that concentrated gaze.

As distracting as it would probably prove to be, having Wil around the house for the next several weeks wouldn't be a hardship. She could certainly think of worse ways to spend her time than watching Wil get sweaty. *What has gotten into me? I've never been so turned on just thinking about someone.*

As she reached the Redmond Diner, Jillian pulled her thoughts away from the attractive contractor. The outside of the building looked like it hadn't had an overhaul in decades.

The painted logo on the front window had long ago faded and begun chipping. When she pushed open the door, the top of the metal frame nudged a small gold bell, announcing her arrival.

"Grab a seat anywhere, honey," a waitress called from across the room.

Jillian slid into one of the vinyl-upholstered booths near the front window. When she noticed a woman she'd seen in the diner before watching her from the next booth, Jillian forced a smile and reminded herself not to react defensively. The small-town curiosity about newcomers took some getting used to.

The woman smiled back and the lines around her mouth deepened. "Make sure you try the apple pie, dear. It's wonderful."

"Thank you."

The woman appeared about Aunt Mary's age. Her neatly pressed paisley blouse was too formal for early afternoon at the diner. Jillian wondered if she had another engagement or if she was simply the type who felt one should always dress to impress when in public no matter what her surroundings. Her white hair was neatly set, and Jillian guessed she had a standing appointment at the salon down the street. She tilted her head and studied Jillian over her menu through a pair of bifocals.

"Aren't you the young lady that's fixing up Mary Connor's place?"

"Yes. I've been here three days. How did you know already?"

"It's a small town, word gets around. I'm Rose Beam."

"Jillian Sealy."

"Would you like to join me for lunch?" Rose gestured to the vacant side of her booth.

Jillian nodded and slid across the worn red vinyl.

"Mary will really be missed," Rose said as she handed Jillian her menu.

"Were you friends?"

"For a time. She was a generous woman." A deep sadness tinged Rose's voice, then just as quickly it was gone. "I hear you're a real-estate agent."

Jillian laughed. "Word really does get around."

"One of the ladies at bingo heard Bud Johnson talking at the hardware store."

While Jillian was still trying to picture a bingo-playing granny hanging out at the hardware store, their waitress approached and they both ordered meatloaf sandwiches and apple pie.

Rose waited until the waitress walked away, then leaned forward and said conspiratorially, "I might have need of your services."

"Well, actually, I'm licensed in Ohio, and since I'm only here for a short time I wasn't planning to apply for my license here."

"Oh." Rose seemed disappointed.

"Are you buying or selling?"

"Selling. I've finally given in and agreed to move closer to my daughter in Virginia. My granddaughter and great-grandchildren live there, as well. There isn't anything left for me here."

"Well, I'm sure there are several good agents in the area." She hadn't seen a real-estate office, but certainly there were others in neighboring towns.

"I shouldn't have bothered you. You probably have a lot of work to do at Mary's place."

Without really knowing why, Jillian wanted to help Rose.

So before she could change her mind, she said, "Maybe I could give you some advice. But I can't collect a commission, and I won't be offended if you want to hire someone else."

"I can't let you work for free."

"Well, I can't take your money."

Rose seemed to be considering her options and then relented. "You stop by tomorrow and I'll show you the house. We'll work something out. Let me just give you the address."

Rose pulled a pen out of her purse and, as she continued to search, Jillian produced one of her business cards and offered the back of it.

In Cincinnati she wouldn't have taken the time to help someone sell a house without the promise of a decent commission. Even if she was so inclined, she wouldn't have had the time. Because a lot of prospective buyers wanted to view property after hours and on weekends, her hours weren't limited to nine to five. And she'd been even busier lately gearing up to sell units in an upscale condominium complex. It was to be her company's biggest project thus far.

Losing that account was one of the things that had compelled her to take on Mary's house.

CHAPTER TWO

Wil walked into the nearly deserted offices of Johnson and Son. Their secretary had taken the day off, and all of their crews were out on jobs. She made a beeline for the coffee urn and hoped her father hadn't been the one to make it. She tested the brew and winced. Bud came from his office as she was adding a healthy dose of creamer.

"Coffee's a little weak," she said sarcastically, just loud enough for him to hear.

"Did you go see Miss Sealy?" He ignored her remark.

Wil pulled a folded invoice from the inside pocket of her denim jacket and handed it to him. "Yesterday. And I just picked up some supplies for her job. Here's the bill. I'll be taking her around to the hardware store later this week to choose some of the custom items."

"What did you think?"

Wil shoved aside the various remarks that sprang to mind regarding Jillian. Her father was asking about the house. "It's a great old place and she has some specific ideas about what she wants done."

"Can your crew get it done in her time frame? I can't spare anyone else."

Wil sensed the challenge in her father's voice. Publicly she knew he supported her and respected her work. But she also suspected on some level he waited for the point when her all-woman crew proved to be less capable than his crews of men. And she took great pleasure in continuing to demonstrate that they were better than the men.

She shoved her shoulders back. "We'll get it done." And they would. If Wil had to work double time to make it happen, the job would come in under Jillian's deadline.

"Good." He poured himself a cup of coffee and drank it undiluted. "We're tying up some big jobs over the summer months, and then I expect a lull in the fall."

Wil nodded. Typically, as early as October, people began budgeting for the holidays instead of home improvement. Business would pick back up in early spring, and by the time it stayed consistently warm they would once again be putting in long hours six days a week. Though it was hectic, Wil didn't mind the schedule. She had a great crew and enjoyed the feeling of accomplishment that came with working until she was too exhausted to do any more.

❖

Jillian grunted as she leaned against the large antique bureau and it barely inched across the hardwood floor. She stopped, fearing she might injure herself or, worse, damage the floor.

"They don't make them like this anymore," she muttered to herself as she slapped her palm against the solid mahogany.

Deciding to leave the dresser until she had some help, she walked over to the stack of boxes she'd started filling that morning. She returned to packing Mary's books, taking a photo album from the half-empty bookcase. The leather cover was worn in places, but obviously well made, and she flipped it open to reveal black-and-white snapshots of Mary's life. A child she guessed was Mary stood outside a church, wearing a dark-colored dress, wide-brimmed hat, and white gloves, her Sunday best. The child held a bunch of wildflowers clasped tight in her right hand, and she smiled widely at whoever was behind the camera.

Prodding herself, Jillian tucked the album in the bureau drawer. She couldn't spend all day looking through photos. Besides, she felt as if she was intruding on Mary's privacy. But there was no one else to tie up the loose ends of Mary's life, so she continued sorting and carefully packing her belongings. That thought saddened her and she couldn't help but wonder who would do this for her someday. While, at thirty-four years old, she was far from spinsterhood, in recent years she had become more aware that she was not where she'd planned to be by this point in her life.

After a string of unfulfilling relationships, she had let her personal life fall by the wayside in favor of her career and told herself that was enough to fulfill her. Her last partner had been unfaithful, then had informed Jillian it was her fault since she cared more about her next commission than their relationship. It had been so long since Jillian had even thought about what she wanted outside of work. She hadn't consciously decided to avoid romance. She had simply continued to make choices based on her opportunities, and it just happened that most of them furthered her career and left less time for social pursuits. But now that her career had taken a new turn or, rather, a drastic detour, she was uncertain. Without the framework of her profession to define her time, she felt directionless.

Thankfully, the sound of the doorbell signaled the end of her self-analysis. And she told herself she was foolish to let a minor setback make her so melancholy. There was nothing wrong with her life a new job won't fix. She'd just been off balance lately and needed to get things back to normal.

She stepped into the main hallway and glanced toward the front door. Through the glass she could see Wil Johnson standing on the porch. Speaking of social pursuits, this woman would sure provide an interesting one.

❖

As the door swung open, Wil stared. Jillian stood framed in the doorway wearing a white tank top and crisp khaki shorts that revealed a sinful length of leg. Her bare limbs glistened with a sheen of sweat, and the strands of hair that escaped her ponytail were damp.

"I've been packing Aunt Mary's things." Jillian seemed flustered. "The movers will be here soon to take them to storage until I figure out what to do with them."

Wil jerked her eyes up and, judging by the flush spreading over Jillian's neck, she guessed she'd been caught staring. She was sure she failed to hide the lust in her eyes, but she found it burning in Jillian's as well, their gold flecks seeming to glow. She dropped her gaze again to Jillian's braless breasts, where her nipples now tented the cotton tank top.

"I have some plans for you," Wil said. *Lord, do I have plans for you.* She held up the folder in her hands. "Um—for the house."

"Sure. Come on in. Can I get you a drink?"

"No, thank you."

Jillian led her to the kitchen. "You've been busy," she said as she went to the refrigerator.

"Yeah, well, when I start a project, I'm committed."

"So what did you bring me?"

Wil watched her take a long pull from a plastic bottle. A trickle of water escaped from the corner of her mouth and ran down her chin and over her neck, accelerated by the muscles in her neck as she swallowed.

When Jillian looked at her expectantly, she opened the folder, laid it on the counter, and consulted her notes. "I thought we could start here in the kitchen since that's where most of the work will be done."

Jillian crossed to stand beside her. "Ah, you're a jump-in-with-both-feet kind of girl, huh?" She leaned to look over Wil's shoulder, and when she did her breast brushed the back of her arm. They both froze, but neither of them acknowledged the contact.

When Wil spoke, her voice was tight. "Normally, no, but in this case it seems appropriate."

Jillian stared at the papers in front of her, unable to look at Wil as she flipped through several sketches and stopped at a floor plan.

"I went over some of your ideas and made a few changes, so I wanted to run them by you before we got started. Here's the new island."

"Okay," she murmured, watching Wil's strong fingers trace a line on the paper. She could imagine those confident hands on her body and a heavy throb began between her thighs, but she forced herself to focus on all the logical reasons why she shouldn't jump her contractor right there in the kitchen. She'd long ago learned it was best to keep working relationships professional. And it had been many years since she'd had a problem sticking to that policy.

"Jillian?" Wil whispered, and Jillian realized she'd been rubbing her breast against Wil's arm.

"Oh, God—I'm sorry." Mortified, she jerked back a step.

But when she would have fled, Wil grabbed her wrist, cupped a hand behind her neck, and kissed her. Her lips were gentle at first, then, when Jillian responded, more aggressive. Wil stroked her tongue silkily inside her mouth and she melted, clutching fistfuls of the back of her shirt.

Wil's mouth was everywhere, sucking her bottom lip, sliding along her jaw, then the side of her neck. Just as frantically, Jillian pulled Wil's T-shirt free from her waistband and shoved both hands under it. She touched the warm skin over Wil's ribs but it wasn't enough. She wanted more.

"This is crazy," she murmured, unsure if she was telling Wil or herself.

"It is," Wil agreed, but she continued to kiss the underside of Jillian's jaw.

I should stop. This time Jillian was certain she didn't speak aloud. Still, it was good advice. But when Wil's fingers slid into her hair at the base of her skull, pleasure spread through her, hot and liquid, and melted her resistance.

"The movers," she practically whimpered as Wil's teeth nipped at her neck. "Don't—have much—time."

"I guess we'll have to be quick," Wil said against her skin, her lips caressing with each word.

With one hand Wil struggled to push her shorts over her hips. Jillian grabbed the waistband and helped shove them down. After she kicked them off, Wil slid her palms against the back of her thighs and lifted her onto the counter.

Desperate to be beneath Wil, Jillian broke the kiss and murmured, "Bedroom?"

"No. Here."

She gasped when Wil cupped her hand against the cotton triangle between her legs. "Ah, you're right. Here is much better." She'd lost the ability to think about anything except having Wil's hands on her. In her. *Now. OhGodnow.*

When Wil squeezed her through her panties, her head swam and she fought the orgasm that threatened to wash over her. *Not yet.*

"Don't. I'll come," she pled when Wil's fingers closed again, milking the pleasure from her flesh.

"It's okay."

She grasped Wil's wrist firmly and stilled her hand. "Not like that. I want you inside."

Wil groaned and, fighting the urge to ignore Jillian's request, pressed her face into Jillian's neck and tried to gather her control. Somehow she knew if she continued to stroke Jillian to a quick climax, she wouldn't resist. "God, you're beautiful," Wil murmured.

Wil shoved aside Jillian's panties and slid inside her. Heat surged between Wil's thighs as warm, wet muscles pulsed around her fingers. Jillian wrapped her legs around her, hooking her heels on the back of Wil's calves, and buried her hands in her hair. She met every thrust, as if the pistoning of her hips could propel her closer to the razor edge of release.

"Harder," Jillian moaned, tugging a fistful of Wil's hair almost to the point of pain. Wil withdrew her fingers almost completely, and when she drove into Jillian, the heel of her hand pounded Jillian's clit. "Oh, yes, that's it."

"Come for me," Wil demanded, as the rasp of Jillian's encouragement and the bite of Jillian's fingernails against her scalp drove her own ascension toward orgasm. "Now." She dragged her tongue across Jillian's collarbone, then bit the silky skin where her shoulder met her neck. Hard. Jillian cried out and, with one final thrust, locked her legs around Wil's hips.

Wil remained inside as the throbbing around her fingers eased.

Jillian sighed and kissed her temple, then her lips. "That was—"

The doorbell rang. Startled, Wil yanked her hand back and Jillian gasped as her fingers slipped out.

"Shit. The movers." Jillian slid to the floor, but her legs were weak and she might have fallen if Wil's arm hadn't come around her waist. She reached between them and fumbled with the fly of her shorts.

"Let me." Propping her against the counter, Wil nudged her hands aside and straightened her clothes. Then she tucked an errant strand of hair behind Jillian's ear. "I'm not finished with you yet," she said, kissing her quickly before taking her shoulders and steering her toward the front door.

Jillian hoped the movers were quick. The feel of Wil's hands was tattooed on her skin, and the promise of more had her trembling as she answered the door.

Since she was going to live in the house for the coming weeks, in addition to furniture in one bedroom, she had elected to keep the sofa in the living room. When she passed through while directing the two men in gray jumpsuits to the dining room, Wil was slouched on the sofa, her knees falling lazily apart and her hands tucked behind her head. Jillian stumbled when she saw the indolent arousal in her eyes.

"Be careful, ma'am," one of the movers said politely, reaching for her elbow.

"Thank you." She flushed with the memory of what they'd been doing when the doorbell rang.

As if reading her mind, Wil smiled and winked at her. Jillian leaned against the door frame between the living room and dining room and tried to look anywhere except at Wil.

"Do you guys need any help?" Wil asked as the two men carried a large oak sideboard toward the front door.

"We've got it," the shorter man replied as they carefully maneuvered it through the front door.

"They've got it," Wil murmured when they were out of earshot. When Jillian glanced at her, she patted the cushion beside her. "You may as well sit down and relax."

"I'm fine." Jillian folded her arms over her chest. She couldn't possibly be within five feet of Wil just then.

Grinning, Wil shifted to the far end of the sofa. "I'll stay at this end and you can sit way down there."

"No, thank you."

Wil's innocent shrug was at odds with her knowing expression. She had to be fully aware of why Jillian kept her distance, and her eyes said she was thinking about the same thing.

By the time the truck was loaded, Jillian was completely avoiding Wil's gloating gaze. Her body hummed with anticipation, but she certainly didn't want the men to read the desire on her face.

"All set, ma'am."

"Thanks, guys." She'd rented a storage unit the day before and had arranged with the storage facility to let the movers unload everything there.

She closed the door, then turned and almost fell against it. Wil didn't move from the sofa but her eyes raked over Jillian's body, and when Jillian crossed the room she had to force herself not to run. She slid one knee on either side of Wil's legs and eased onto her lap, straddling her.

"I thought they'd never leave," Wil murmured, bringing her hands to Jillian's hips.

"You were looking at me as if you weren't going to wait until they left."

Wil ran her hands under her T-shirt and cupped her full

breasts. “I’m not into having an audience.” She rubbed her thumbs over erect nipples, stopped, and tilted her head in question. Then she lightly pinched Jillian’s right nipple, feeling the bar that passed through it.

Jillian gasped at the slight tug and smiled. “Youthful indiscretion,” she said by way of explanation.

“I want to see.” Realizing she had been in such a hurry earlier that she hadn’t found the piercing, Wil vowed to go slower this time.

Jillian pulled up her T-shirt, baring her right breast. Experimentally, Wil played with the small silver balls resting on either side of her nipple. She was fascinated by the piercing that seemed so out of character. Equally interesting was the way Jillian trembled and her breathing quickened as she toyed with the jewelry. Wil drew her shirt over her head and lightly bit her nipple.

“I have a confession,” Jillian said, her back arching as Wil’s tongue flicked against the piercing. Wil cradled Jillian’s shoulder blades in her hands, bent over her, and continued to work the hardened nipple with her teeth and tongue.

“What’s that?”

“Earlier, when you were talking about your plans for the house”—she rolled her hips hard in Wil’s lap and watched her eyes go hazy—“I didn’t hear a thing you said.” Straightening, she braced her hands on the back of the sofa on either side of Wil’s head.

“I’ll go over it again later.” Wil worked open her fly. “Or you could just trust in my considerable skill.”

Jillian threaded her fingers into Wil’s hair, pulled her head back, then raked her teeth over Wil’s neck. “Having experienced your skills firsthand, I think I’d like a more… thorough demonstration.”

“Oh, I can definitely do that.” Wil returned her mouth to

Jillian's full breast and toyed lightly with a pebbled nipple. When she sucked it gently, Jillian's hips ground restlessly against the tops of her thighs.

"Please, Wil. *Do* something."

Wil flipped her onto her back on the sofa, all thoughts of going slow fleeing at Jillian's plea. After she'd helped her remove her shorts and panties, she pulled her back into her lap, wrapped her arms around her waist, and pressed closer. With a hand under Wil's chin, Jillian guided her face up for a bruising kiss. In the not-so-gentle bite of teeth against tender lips and the aggressive stroke of tongues, they traded control while adding fuel to the arousal that flared hotly between them.

Wil led, kneading Jillian's breasts, then followed when Jillian gripped one of her wrists and guided her hand between her legs. Obeying Jillian's urging, Wil slid her fingers home, reveling in the feel of slick muscles gripping her and Jillian's low moan.

Her nerve endings screaming for gratification, Jillian rose up on her knees until only Wil's fingertips remained inside, then drove her hips downward, engulfing her again.

"More," she whispered, and Wil slipped another finger alongside the others.

Bracing her hands on Wil's shoulders, she set an increasing rhythm. Blinding pleasure spiraled inside her with each thrust as she forced Wil's fingers deeper. She raced onward, uncertain if she was rushing toward release or trying to outrun it. But when Wil moved her other hand between them and circled her thumb over her straining clitoris, she felt the first wave. Then she could no longer stay ahead of the curl as it barreled over her, swirling her in a wash of ecstasy. The erratic jerk of her hips eased to a slow roll in an effort to draw the last bit of pleasure from her sensitive flesh before she allowed Wil to withdraw.

Jillian slumped forward and rested her forehead on Wil's shoulder. Panting, she pressed her mouth to the salty skin of Wil's neck.

Wil traced her fingers lightly along the curve of Jillian's spine, apparently content to bask in Jillian's pleasure. But Jillian had other ideas as she dragged her tongue up the side of Wil's neck. She slid off her lap, knelt in front of her, and tugged open her button fly. Wil lifted her hips and Jillian eased her jeans off, then pulled her closer to the edge of the sofa. She caressed the inside of her thighs, pressing them apart. When she lowered herself to kiss the warm skin beneath her hands, the scent of Wil's arousal drew her fingertips upward, and she was compelled to feel the wetness she knew she'd find there.

She met Wil's eyes as she caressed into hot, slippery folds. Slumped against the back of the sofa, Wil watched her, azure eyes filled with such need that Jillian shivered, never having been the subject of such intensity.

Wil touched Jillian's cheek, then as Jillian bowed her head, Wil's fingers slipped into her hair. Jillian circled her tongue lightly around Wil's clitoris, teasing, and Wil raised her hips seeking more. With a forearm across her pelvis, Jillian held her down, continuing the light strokes.

"Please, I won't last long," Wil ground out, straining against Jillian's arm. "Baby, please, suck me." Before she'd finished her plea, Jillian took her fully in her mouth. "Ah, that's it."

Seconds later, as Wil's flesh pulsed against her lips and tongue, she dropped a hand to stroke between her own thighs. Once, then again, harder, and she tripped over the edge behind Wil.

Chapter Three

Jillian awoke early, as she did every morning. But the difference today was the warm body against her bare back and Wil's arm circling her waist. She felt surprisingly rested considering she'd spent most of the previous afternoon and night crawling all over the woman lying next to her.

She rolled onto her back and Wil stirred beside her. Staying professional had never been a problem for her before, but she'd been completely unable to manage it where Wil was concerned. She could just imagine what her friends would say if they found out she'd slept with Wil. She didn't consider them snobs, but she knew in this case they would feel an affair with a contractor was beneath her. And she would have agreed. Though she certainly wasn't a prude, jumping into bed with someone she had just met wasn't like her either. But, the devil on her shoulder reminded her, sticking to her norm had never led to the incredible sex she'd had last night.

She trailed her fingers over Wil's bare shoulder. The skin there was pale, and the deep tan of her forearms, likely the result of hours spent working in the sun, began in the center of her bicep. A thin scar started at her elbow, ran down her arm, and ended at her wrist. A collection of smaller nicks peppered her hands, reminders of how different they were. In comparison, Jillian's own hand was smooth and well tended, thanks to regular manicures.

She wondered if Wil was a late sleeper and realized she didn't know anything about her. She didn't know how she took her coffee. Hell, she didn't even know if she drank coffee.

"What are you thinking about so hard?" Wil murmured. Her arm was still draped across Jillian's midsection and she caressed her hip.

"How did you know I was thinking?"

Wil raised up on her elbow and shoved a lock of dark hair off her forehead. "You get a little wrinkle between your eyebrows when you're concentrating. I noticed it yesterday when you were giving me the tour."

Jillian smiled and touched Wil's bare chest just above a small, firm breast. Regardless of what she speculated her friends would think, even they couldn't deny Wil's attractiveness. Her blue eyes were clear and made even more brilliant by her tanned skin. The slight swells of her breasts and hips were the only hint of softness on her work-hardened body. And her wicked grin made her damn near irresistible. "I don't know how much experience you have with women, Wil. But where I come from, telling a woman she has a wrinkle is not considered flattery."

Wil laughed and Jillian felt the vibration beneath her palm. "Well, we do things a bit differently in the South."

"Do you, now?" Jillian smoothed her hand down Wil's stomach but Wil caught it and cradled it against her chest.

"You wore me out last night, Jillian."

"Not a morning person?" Again, Wil's accented voice caressing her name made Jillian's libido tug at her wayward self-control.

Wil lay back and gathered Jillian against her. After marathon sex the night before, she'd finally fallen into an exhausted slumber, and this morning she wanted to linger in that afterglow. "Do you really think you can have this house ready to sell in five weeks?"

"Don't you?"

"If you bust your ass." Wil playfully squeezed the ass in question. "You must be in a hurry to get back home."

"It probably seems that way. And I'm not even sure why. It's not like I have much to go back to." Jillian's head rested on Wil's shoulder and she absently drew figure eights on the center of her chest.

"What do you mean?"

"I quit my job three days before I found out about Aunt Mary's passing."

"You didn't have anything else lined up?" Wil couldn't imagine resigning without the security of another position. Then again, Wil was pretty much invested in Johnson and Son, since someday her father would hand over the reins.

Jillian's fingers drifted across her breast, closer to her nipple, distracting her.

"I didn't know I'd need to. I'd been there for seven years and had the highest sales in the company for the past six. Then my boss gave the biggest deal we've ever had to his idiot son-in-law."

"So you quit?"

Jillian laughed bitterly. "I gave him an ultimatum. I marched into his office and told him either he would give me what I deserved or I was quitting. He told me to be out by the end of the day."

"Ouch."

"Yeah. Three days later I was here. Since I have some experience with home design and what buyers are looking for, I figured I might as well take the time to fix the house up a bit first."

Jillian's index finger brushed Wil's nipple and she shivered. She'd spent the better part of the night responding to Jillian's ardent caresses, but this casual contact, seemingly not intended to arouse, affected her just as strongly.

Apparently not noticing her reaction, Jillian continued to talk. "Then when I got here I fell in love with the place. I'll admit it's a bit of a dream to have free rein over this house."

"You have a great eye. If you don't find another job in real estate, you could always flip a few houses. There's plenty of money to be made in that."

"We'll see how much fun I've had by the time I finish this one. I won't have trouble finding a job with another firm. I'm sure when word gets around that I'm available, I'll have plenty of offers." She made another pass over Wil's nipple.

"What? You're not having fun here?"

"Oh, I'm having fun."

The third time she skimmed over the puckered flesh, Wil suspected it was deliberate. The mischievous look in her eye confirmed it.

"Are you?" She bent her head to capture Jillian's mouth, purposely lingering. She traced her supple lips before stroking her tongue between them.

"Oh, yes. Very much." Jillian felt Wil responding to her touch and her own body surged with awareness of what Wil looked like when she climaxed, the flush on her chest and neck, the way her eyelids closed almost reverently, and the hoarse cry that carried Jillian's name with it. She slipped her leg over Wil's hips and rose to straddle her. "But right now, I've got to get up, because I have an appointment this morning."

She slid off her, letting the length of her body rub against Wil's. She smiled as she carefully skirted Wil's reaching hand.

"Tease." Wil didn't move from thc bed.

"I told Rose Beam I would give her some advice about selling her house. So I'm going over to see it and discuss her asking price." Jillian grabbed a silk robe from the chair nearby.

"She's selling?" Wil folded her arms behind her head and watched Jillian move around the room gathering clean clothes.

"Surprised?"

"Yes, actually. She's lived in that house for—well, longer than I've been alive. Before her daughter moved to Virginia, I went to school with her granddaughter."

"Is Rose a widow?"

"No. She never married." Wil sat up. "If you don't mind letting me grab a shower, I'll drive you."

"That's not necessary."

"I haven't seen Miss Rose in months," she said. "Besides, if she's selling, she'll need to fix a few things up. So she'll probably hire us anyway since we've done work for her before."

"Okay, if you're sure she won't mind."

"I'm sure." When Jillian passed within reach, Wil grabbed her hand and drew her to the edge of the bed. "And we can conserve water if you shower with me."

"So you're concerned about my water bill?"

"If it will get us wet together, sure I am."

"Oh, I'm quite certain we won't have any trouble getting wet together." Jillian stood and untied her robe. As she headed for the bathroom, she let it fall to the floor. "Hurry up, stud, we don't have much time."

❖

Their shower took a bit longer than expected, because as it turned out Wil was a morning person after all. And by the time they both toweled themselves dry, her legs shook and her head was filled with steamy images of pressing Jillian against the shower wall and kneeling before her.

Jillian gave her a clean T-shirt, and she pulled on the jeans she'd worn the night before. When Jillian crossed the room in only her bra and panties, Wil paused in the midst of buttoning her fly. The curve of Jillian's waist flared at the hips and a triangle of pale pink cotton clung to her shapely ass. Suddenly overcome with the desire to pass her lips over the back of Jillian's thighs, she debated stripping her jeans off and trying to convince Jillian that they didn't have to go just yet. She wondered why it felt so good to torture herself and stood there and watched as Jillian covered those delicious expanses of skin.

After they finished dressing, she waited while Jillian locked up, then followed her down the walk. She would have opened the passenger door, but Jillian was around the front of the truck and climbing into the cab before she could. So she slid behind the wheel and started the engine.

"I still can't believe Miss Rose is selling," she said, but Jillian only murmured absently in response, seeming to be too distracted for conversation.

Jillian wondered how it was possible that even the way Wil drove was sexy, her hand draped lazily over the wheel. Seriously. She thought she'd be well past the stage in her life where she could get hormonal over a woman. But even after a night that should have left her sated, she was sitting here imagining what Wil would do if she climbed onto her lap and—*okay, enough. That's quite enough of that.* Aware she was riding down Main Street in a truck with a logo on the side, she decided she should wait at least a full week before she started a town scandal.

What was she thinking? Was she really going to have a fling with her contractor? Well, it was too late to ask that question, since essentially she'd already begun it. Wasn't that what this was—a fling? Well, so what if it was? Shouldn't she just enjoy it for whatever it ended up being? She'd spent all of her life planning for the future, and it was about time she lived in the now for a change. What better time than when she had no plans whatsoever and a gorgeous prospect sitting inches away. Her life had been absolutely derailed when she'd lost her job, and she'd pounced on the opportunity to come to Redmond and sell the house. Now that she'd set a precedent for spontaneous change, she might as well continue it.

She glanced out the window as Wil pulled to the curb in front of a stone cottage-style home. The porch tucked under the low roof sagged, and one of the oversized green wood shutters flanking each narrow, arched window hung lopsided.

She got out of the car and studied the house, making mental notes. This was the first impression a buyer would get, and it was important to dress it up if they hoped to get anyone to look at the inside. The shrubs in front of the house were in desperate need of pruning, and some path lights would dress up the walk. A low stone retaining wall followed the length of the property line, and the creeping phlox that blanketed it had run rampant.

"You need to shore up that porch," she murmured as Wil joined her and they walked up the stone path.

"Okay. Listen, Rose has lived here for more than half her life. Be gentle with the criticism."

"I *have* handled this type of situation before." She bristled at Wil's attempt to tell her how to do her job. She didn't get where she was by being insensitive to her clients' needs. People took criticism about their homes personally, and, while she didn't let that deter her from delivering an objective assessment, she was considerate of that fact.

"Of course, I didn't mean to imply—"

Wil fell silent when Rose appeared on the porch.

"Good morning," she called. Her eyes moved between the two of them, and Jillian suddenly realized Wil stood very close and her hand lightly touched the small of her back. "It's lovely to see you again, Jillian."

"It's very nice to see you too."

Rose turned to Wil. "Wilhelmina, it's been too long. How is your mother?"

"She's well, Miss Rose. She's still living in D.C. with my stepfather."

"Come inside, girls."

Behind Rose's back, Jillian whispered, "Wilhelmina?"

"My mother's idea," she mumbled.

Jillian giggled, but as Wil's expression hardened she choked her response off. "I'm sorry. It's a wonderful name."

"But it doesn't exactly fit me. Does it?" When Wil straightened, hooked her thumb through her belt loop, and thrust her shoulders back, Jillian was struck by the aggressive sexuality she exuded.

"Not really."

Rose held the door open for them. "I made lemonade and sugar cookies."

"Miss Rose, how do you always manage to make me feel like I'm twelve years old again?" Wil climbed the steps to the porch.

Jillian tried to imagine Wil as a twelve-year-old girl and immediately pictured a gangly tomboy in ripped jeans and an old T-shirt. Was Wil always tall, or did she have a growth spurt during her teenage years?

"You spent as much time over here as you did at home that summer."

The front door opened into a small foyer and Rose led them to a spacious kitchen. The linoleum was yellowed and the white cabinets needed a coat of paint. Actually, they needed to be replaced, but Jillian wasn't sure what Rose's budget was. The appliances were outdated—in fact, she guessed the fridge was circa 1950—but she didn't think replacing them would gain that much value for the house. Besides, vintage was in again.

"Nancy and I were inseparable." A smile softened by reminiscence touched Wil's lips.

"Nancy is my granddaughter," Rose said to Jillian as she took three glasses from the cabinet. To Wil she said, "Get the pitcher from the refrigerator, dear."

"Then the next summer I started working for Dad."

Jillian watched as Wil's face took on a stubborn sadness. "Wasn't that also around the time your parents split up?"

"Yeah." Jillian thought she saw a look of understanding pass between them.

After a sympathetic smile, Rose changed the subject. "It's such a nice day. Let's sit on the back porch."

Rose carried a plate of cookies and they followed with the lemonade and glasses.

Behind the house a large oak tree cast shade over most of the moderately sized yard, which would provide space for children to play and would be a selling point for potential buyers. The surprisingly large porch held a cedar table and chairs. A flower box on the railing was overflowing with lush purple flowers that Jillian couldn't identify.

Wil pulled out a chair for her and, as she sat, Wil's hands brushed across the top of her shoulders to tease the bare skin of her neck.

"It's good to see the two of you together," Rose said.

"We're not—I mean—we didn't. Wil is doing some work on Aunt Mary's house for me." Responding both to the ripple of pleasure along her spine at Wil's touch and to something she thought she'd heard in Rose's tone, Jillian rushed to explain her presence and felt Wil stiffen beside her.

"Of course, dear. Thank you for bringing her along on your visit. I would have called her father after our meeting anyway," Rose said calmly. If she noticed Jillian's discomfort, she'd obviously chosen to ignore it.

While Rose served the lemonade, Jillian outlined some of her suggestions. Rose once again offered compensation for her time, but since Jillian wasn't licensed in Tennessee, she didn't feel right accepting.

"Well, then at least let me make you dinner tomorrow night."

Jillian held up a cookie. "If these are any indication of your culinary skills, I accept."

"I thought you might. You've been eating too many meals down at the diner. You need a good home-cooked meal."

She grinned. "I'm not really very good in the kitchen. And I enjoy the nightly walks through town to the diner."

Rose looked at Wil, who toyed with her half-empty glass, tracing her fingers through the condensation on the outside. "Wil, you're welcome too, of course."

"Thank you, but I already have plans."

To Jillian, Wil's reply sounded false, but Rose seemed to accept it easily.

"Come by if your plans change. It sounds as if I'll need

help with some of these projects. Would you ask your father to call me when he has someone free?"

"I can fit you in between work on Mary's place." Though Wil's mind was elsewhere, she had been half listening to Jillian and Rose talk about getting the house ready to sell. She had to admit, Jillian had handled the suggested changes delicately and seemed sensitive to Rose's limited income.

"Oh, I don't want to interfere with your other work."

She waved off Rose's concern. "My crew can handle some of the work over there without me. I'll squeeze yours in between supervising them." She could feel Jillian's eyes on her but didn't look at her. She'd caught Jillian's nervousness when she'd misinterpreted Rose's comment about the two of them. And she'd very quickly understood from where Jillian's reaction stemmed. So now she jumped on the excuse to be away from the job site at Mary's place whenever possible.

❖

Wil strode out to her truck and Jillian hurried to keep up. She barely managed to slide into the passenger seat before Wil accelerated away from the curb.

"Is something wrong?" She touched Wil's arm.

"No." Wil jerked her arm away and gripped the wheel with both hands.

For several silent moments, Wil tested the strength of the seat belts, careening around a corner and screeching to a halt at a stop sign. Jillian's body lurched forward until the belt caught and locked almost painfully across her chest.

"Jesus, what is your problem?"

"I don't have a problem. As long as I remember my place."

"What the hell are you talking about?" Jillian didn't have a clue what had set Wil off, but from the harsh bite in her voice and the firm set of her jaw, she was plenty mad.

"You were pretty quick to make it clear I was *just* an employee."

"That's ridiculous." Was Wil joking? Maybe Jillian simply didn't know her personality well enough to tell. If she was, she deserved an Oscar for this performance because she looked livid.

"Is it? You overreacted to Rose's statement. Would it be that horrible if Rose figured out that there was something going on between us?"

"This isn't personal. But I don't need this whole town gossiping about what I'm doing with—"

"The handyman?"

"Now who's overreacting?" Jillian muttered. The derision in Wil's voice hit home and Jillian was getting angry too. After last night, she'd thought they were on the same page. It was just sex. Surely Wil could see that's all they could share. Hell, she was only here for a short time anyway. She'd thought they were both adults and could merely enjoy each other, but here Wil was blowing everything out of proportion.

"I just don't think Miss Rose is the type to gossip. Especially—"

She waited, but Wil didn't continue. "What?"

"Nothing."

Frustrated, she shook her head. "Look, I just didn't want her to assume there's anything going on between us."

"I don't think she assumed anything."

"Wil, please don't make this difficult."

Wil pulled the truck up to the curb in front of her house and slammed the gearshift into Park.

Jillian tried again. “Wcll, is there something wrong with wanting to appear professional?”

Wil scowled. “That’s not what this was about. You’re worried about what people will think about you *doing* the hired help.”

“How darc you presume to know what I’m thinking. You don’t know me.” Wil had hit closer to the truth than Jillian was willing to admit.

“You’re right. I don’t.” Wil threw up her hands and stared out the windshield. “And that’s precisely why I shouldn’t have fucked you.”

Jillian flinched at Wil’s blunt language, even though moments ago she’d also reduced their encounter to just that.

“It’s okay, Miss Sealy.” Wil’s expression was blank, her voice emotionless. “I’m quite used to being seen as a second-class citizen in this town.”

“Wil—”

“Get out.”

“I just want—”

“Get. Out. Of my truck.”

She sighed and shoved the door open. As soon as her feet hit the ground, she slammed the door behind her. She didn’t turn around, but seconds later she heard gravel fly as Wil sped away.

CHAPTER FOUR

Wil pulled a beer from the refrigerator and resisted the urge to slam the door. She tossed the cap in the sink on her way to the attached garage. After she flipped on the light, she set the bottle on the workbench where her tools were laid out neatly just inside the door. In the center of the garage, the makeshift table she'd fashioned out of a sheet of plywood and two sawhorses held four drawers. She'd finished assembling them the night before for a rolltop desk she was making for her father's office. Tonight she would begin cutting the pieces for the base.

Six years ago, after she bought this house on fifteen acres on the town's outskirts, she had transformed the garage into a workshop. A decade old, the house was more modern and sterile than she liked. As subdivisions crawled out from nearby cities, construction companies had begun to build cookie-cutter houses, and Wil's was no exception. She'd been more interested in the land than the house. But the relatively cheap cost of maintaining the small home allowed her to save until she built the house she really wanted.

Still, it was much nicer than the place her family had lived in when she was younger. Bud had been struggling to rebuild the company that her grandfather, with a series of bad business decisions, had nearly run into the ground. They had rented a dilapidated house that probably should have been condemned years ago. Bud made what repairs he could with no money, but the house needed major work.

Wil knew her mother wasn't happy. She heard them arguing when they thought she was asleep. Her mother screamed at her father that her college education was wasted while she waited tables at the diner. She hated living in a small town and wanted to move back to D.C. where she had grown up. He usually tried to convince her that things would get better, but one night when Wil was twelve years old, he told her to go. And she did. Wil remembered standing in front of the house watching her drive away. Her mother had tried to explain why she was leaving, but Wil was too hurt and angry to listen and ignored her until she finally gave up and got in the car.

After that Bud had taken nearly any job he could just to keep food on the table. And still Wil had gone to school many days with no lunch money, in clothes from Goodwill. In such a small town, that meant the other kids recognized their own discarded, season-old clothing.

Wil took pride in owning her home because no one had ever expected anything from her. She and Bud had worked hard, and Johnson and Son now had a reputation for quality work and dependability. But she suspected many residents would always view her as the poor girl in secondhand clothes. She'd seen more than her share of pitying looks from her elders over the years.

This afternoon had proved that a part of her that could still be stung by an offhand remark. Jillian Sealy was white-collar, and not just by profession. Her carriage and the confidence with which she made eye contact communicated the expectation that she would be treated a certain way. Despite Wil's occasional arrogance, she would never have that sense of entitlement. She knew she would always be susceptible to the resurgence of childhood shame, and Jillian's quick reaction to Rose's harmless remark had stirred that old inadequacy.

She would probably do best to remember that her relationship with Jillian was strictly professional. They'd lost their heads for one passionate evening, but she could put things back on track. Hell, she'd had a six-month relationship with Andy, one of her crew members, a while back, and they still managed to work together. She had a job to do, and Jillian had made it plain that her plans for them didn't include anything more than that.

"Yep, keep it professional," she muttered to herself as she drained the rest of her beer. She put on her safety glasses and set the guard on the saw. Burying herself in measurements and sawdust was one way to clear her mind.

❖

"No, I don't know when I'll be home." Propped against the kitchen counter, Jillian wedged her cell phone between her cheek and shoulder while she filed her nails. Monica, her friend and fellow real-estate agent in Cincinnati, had called to check on her when she hadn't heard from her in several days.

"I thought you were just going down there to sell the house," Monica said.

"Well, I was. But there's a lot to be done before it's ready to list. Besides, I don't have a job to rush home to."

"You could get your old job back."

"I refuse to beg that asshole to rehire me." Jillian applied light pink polish to her thumbnail, then debated whether she liked the shade.

"I can talk to my boss."

"Monica, I'm not worried. I'm sure I could call any number of firms."

"If you want to get on with a good firm, you shouldn't stay away too long. Real estate is fickle."

"As soon as things are sorted here."

"I'd think you would be in a hurry. There can't be much in Hicktown to stick around for."

Jillian immediately recalled the hazy look of passion in Wil's eyes.

"Jillian?"

"What?" She shivered at the memory of Wil whispering her name.

"Am I missing something?"

"No." She shook her head as if she could clear Wil's face from her mind as easily as an Etch-a-Sketch screen. "No. If I take a few weeks and fix the place up, I can make a nice profit."

"A few weeks? Jillian, get your ass up here while people still remember your name."

"Don't be so dramatic. The market will still be there when I get back. Maybe I'll think about starting my own firm." She'd planned on going out on her own in about five years anyway. She would just be accelerating that schedule.

After finishing her nails, she carefully recapped the polish and waved her hands to dry. A knock at the door gave her an excuse to end the conversation. "Someone's here. I'll call you in a few days."

She hung up before Monica could protest. When she swung open the door, Wil stood on the porch, staring out at the street.

"Hello, Wil." After the way they'd left things the day

before, Jillian was surprised to see her. From the little she knew about her, she'd expected it would take a few more days for Wil to come around asking for forgiveness.

Wil faced her, shoved her hands in the back pockets of her jeans, and rocked on her heels. Her eyes were hidden by dark sunglasses and her expression was stony.

"We need to go to the hardware store if we're going to get your kitchen fixtures ordered in time."

Expecting an apology, Jillian blinked, taken off guard by her lack of contrition.

"I didn't call," Wil said abruptly.

"What?"

"I didn't call. So if this is a bad time I can come back later."

"Um—no. Now is fine."

She grabbed her coat and purse from the hook behind the door, locked up, and followed Wil to her truck. It was only a couple of blocks to the hardware store, and if they hadn't been picking up supplies she would have suggested they walk rather than get in Wil's truck again. Instead she climbed silently into the cab, staying as close to the door as she could. Beneath the scent of sawdust and paint thinner, she picked up the clean, light scent of Wil's cologne and cursed her awareness. She didn't need drama, and if that's what Wil was after, Jillian should get over her attraction very quickly. But considering the tension in the truck, it would be a long five weeks if she continued to be this physically conscious of Wil.

"I assume, since my father didn't fire me this morning, you didn't call him." Jillian sensed a touch of challenge beneath Wil's icy tone.

"No."

She'd considered it, but couldn't think of a plausible

reason to request a different crew. And she couldn't imagine telling Bud Johnson the real reason she didn't want to work with his daughter. Out of curiosity, she had contacted another contractor, but they wouldn't have a crew available for another three weeks. So she was left with little choice but to stick it out with Wil.

"I'm an adult, Wil. I see no reason to mess with your livelihood just because you and I had a misunderstanding."

Wil laughed humorlessly. "A misunderstanding? Is that what we're calling it?"

"Well, that would be the civilized way to handle things." Jillian could have said she was sorry. But stubbornly she refused, not wanting to be the first to apologize.

"Of course." Wil's expression was blank. She wheeled into the lot in front of Bill's Hardware, parked, and jumped out without another word.

Jillian felt like she'd been transported back in time as she followed Wil through the wood-framed screen door. Merchandise covered the walls, each of the six aisles, and nearly every available surface of the small store. A long counter across the front of the store held an antiquated cash register and stacks of catalogs. She wandered down the nearest aisle, passing bins with nails, bolts, and screws of every size. On the back wall she found a complete palette of paint samples arranged in a rack lit with fluorescent bulbs.

She selected several of the small cards in colors she liked and tucked them in her purse. She'd never actually painted a room, but she'd picked up a few home-improvement magazines and decided it sounded simple enough. The interior paint had gone on her list and she'd put the exterior paint on Wil's.

"We won't be ready for you to paint anything for at least a week," Wil said from behind her.

"I know. But I want to take some samples home and consider them. I like this green for the kitchen. And this one for the dining room."

"It's yellow." Wil's distaste was evident in her tone.

"You don't like yellow?"

"Ah, it's not my favorite."

"But it's not an obnoxious shade. And it will look perfect with the white trim and really reflect the light in that room."

"Hey, it's your house." Wil raised her hands in surrender.

"Well, it's really not." Jillian replaced the rich ochre and selected beige instead. "And it's better to stick with less dramatic colors when trying to sell." She recited the advice she'd given numerous clients.

"Have you given any thought to an exterior color?"

"I guess I shouldn't suggest yellow."

Wil rolled her eyes and took Jillian's elbow, seeming not to notice when Jillian started at the contact. "Come over here and look at these kitchen cabinets."

Jillian shivered, unable, even after Wil released her, to banish the sensory memory of her touch. And it irritated her that Wil seemed unaffected as she led her to a display of varying types and shades of wood samples.

Wil flipped open a catalog on the counter in front of her, and once against Jillian found herself watching Wil's hands. She remembered the feel of them grasping her hips, guiding her as she thrust against her.

"I think you should choose something of average price, very neutral."

She forced herself to pay attention to the cabinets Wil pointed out, hoping that concentrating on business would calm her storming senses. Shutting out Wil's light scent and the warmth of her body so close, Jillian focused on the pages in front of her. She'd intended the kitchen to be attractive yet economical, but as they leafed through the catalog, she noticed the products she'd want in her own home.

"I want these. In white." She pointed out a set with frosted glass inserts in the upper cabinets. "Dark countertops. Granite, maybe, or engineered stone."

Wil shook her head. "Too expensive."

"These are the ones I want," Jillian insisted, annoyed by Wil's quick dismissal.

"Then compromise on the countertop. We can do tile cheaper."

"I like granite."

"I thought you wanted to make a profit. If you don't prioritize you'll never get back what you put into it."

Wil's confidence grated against Jillian's already tender nerves, and when she responded her tone was harsher than she intended. "Suddenly, you're an expert on real estate."

Wil stared at her for a moment and she wished she could identify the emotion that flashed quickly in those brilliant blue eyes. "No. But I know something about remodeling."

"Well, it's my project. Order these," she punctuated her words with a jab at the page, "and the granite."

While Wil wordlessly copied the product information, Jillian opened another catalog. She immediately noticed a beautiful brushed-nickel kitchen faucet whose clean, modern lines would go perfectly with the cabinets she'd just chosen. One glance at the price told her that she'd be pushing Wil if she insisted on ordering it. Instead she found a cheaper model and reminded herself that she planned to sell the house when she was done anyway. She chose a similar set for the bathroom sinks.

"We're putting the new shower in the master. It'll need

fixtures as well," Wil said as she added the ones Jillian indicated to her list. "Do you have any ideas about the tile in there?"

"Do I need to decide that now?"

"We won't start the bathroom until we're done in the kitchen. But if Bill has to order it, he does need some lead time."

Jillian thought varying shades of gray tile would complement the slate blue she wanted for the walls. Coupled with the glass shower, and the nickel fixtures, the overall effect would be clean and elegant. She tried to concentrate on the image of the finished bathroom instead of the feel of Wil's breath against her neck as she leaned over her shoulder to look at the catalog. When Wil brushed against her back, she fought the memory of what had happened in the kitchen when their positions had been reversed.

"We'll start demolition Monday morning. I've arranged for a Dumpster to be delivered. My girls will be there at eight."

"Your girls?"

"My crew. Three of the hardest-working women you'll ever find." Wil started toward the front of the store. As they reached the counter, she called, "Bill, we're ready."

A young man pushed through the half door from what Jillian assumed was an office. He looked around Wil's age, a few years younger than Jillian, she guessed. His sandy hair was shaggy, and he wore a faded black Scorpions T-shirt and worn jeans. When he took Wil's list and turned to enter it in a compact laptop Jillian hadn't noticed before, she saw the distinctive shape of a Skoal can in his back pocket. This wasn't how she'd pictured the "Bill" in Bill's Hardware. For some reason she imagined an older man in flannel and suspenders.

"All set, Wil." He handed back her list and a receipt. "I haven't seen you down at the Ranch lately."

Wil shrugged. "You know how it is, we're busy."

"Me too. Ever since Granddaddy passed, I've been running this place by myself. But you gotta let off some steam sometimes."

"The ranch?" Jillian wondered how working on a ranch could be relaxing.

"Rambles Ranch is a bar on the west side of town. You probably drove by it on your way in," Wil explained.

Jillian recalled passing the wood-shingled building that resembled a bunkhouse. She hadn't paid attention to the name stenciled on a sign outside, but the glowing neon beer signs in the windows had made its purpose clear.

"You oughta hire one of the high-school boys to help out nights and weekends." Wil folded her receipt and shoved it in her jacket pocket.

Bill shrugged. "I've got one part-time guy already. And my brother will be home from college next week. He'll help out for the summer."

"Well, try not to work too hard," Wil said as she led Jillian out of the store.

"I guess there are a lot of family-owned businesses in this town," Jillian commented as they walked to the truck.

"There's not much in the way of jobs around town. So if you grow up here and want to stick around, you either commute to the city or go into the family business. Most places have been in the same family for generations."

"Like Bill's."

Wil slid behind the wheel and started the truck. "Yep. His grandfather, the one he's named after, opened the hardware store about the same time mine started Johnson and Son. Bill's father took off when he and his brother were young, but Bill has been working there since we were in high school."

Jillian suspected there were several parallels between Bill's life and Wil's. Except from what she'd gathered, it was Wil's mother who had left. She recalled the flash of sadness when Rose mentioned her parents' split.

"Were you and Bill good friends?"

"Oh, yeah. After Nancy moved away, Billy was my only friend for a while."

"Really?" Though Wil's tone was light, it felt false, and Jillian could sense the loneliness she tried to cover. Wil was attractive and magnetic, and Jillian had difficulty imagining her so solitary.

Wil's right hand rested on the gearshift between them, her other draped over the steering wheel, and she stared straight ahead. "Yeah. I went to school with the same kids from kindergarten on. You wouldn't think it would matter how much money my family had. Or didn't have."

"It was really a big deal? This doesn't seem like the type of town where wealth is important. It's too idyllic."

"It's not Mayberry. We have our share of problems."

Jillian laughed. "Yeah, like what? There's no traffic, no crime, everyone knows everyone else—"

"Exactly. So everybody was fully aware that, while my classmates were shopping and hanging out at the diner all summer, I was building additions to their houses, putting on new roofs, and unstopping their toilets. Because, after all, nothing was beneath us at Johnson and Son."

Wil bitterly ground out her last words, then clenched her jaw shut, a muscle jumping with the effort.

"And look at you now."

"Most of the time, I don't feel any different than I did then."

Jillian didn't understand the point in holding on to that

past resentment. If someone didn't think she was good enough, well—screw them. She knew who she was, and she'd never let anyone convince her otherwise.

Chapter Five

"Are you sure I can't do something to help?" Jillian called from a chair at Rose's dining-room table. Though it was just the two of them, Rose had laid out matching white chinaware and polished silver on the starched linen tablecloth.

Rose entered from the kitchen with a bowl of mashed potatoes. "That's okay, dear, I've got it."

"At least let me carry something." When she returned to the kitchen, Jillian followed.

"Okay, I'll get the dinner rolls from the oven. You take this." Rose handed her a platter piled with thick slices of roast beef.

"You have a beautiful home. You must have many happy memories here," Jillian said as they sat down.

Rose smiled. "Yes. We had some lovely times. But the marks of my daughter's growth on the bedroom doorjamb and the loose board in the hallway that creaked every time she tried to sneak out aren't exactly big selling points."

"Well, I think they are. Not in the traditional sense, maybe. But this house has history, and with that beautiful yard out back, your target buyer is a young family who will make their own memories."

"That's nice of you to say."

They passed dishes back and forth until both of their plates were filled. The aroma of roast beef and rich gravy mingled with fresh-baked rolls that Jillian would bet were made from scratch.

"Are you looking forward to spending more time with your family?" Jillian took a bite. "This is delicious."

"Yes. I have three great-grandchildren. And for so many years it was just my daughter and I. It will be nice to have family around."

"It must have been difficult raising a child on your own."

Despite a few rough patches, Jillian's parents were still together, and she couldn't imagine her mother trying to cope alone. Her parents had sacrificed a lot of time to provide her and her brother with their upper-middle-class lifestyle. As a surgeon, her father had been away often during her upbringing, leaving her mother, an obstetrician, with the bulk of the child-rearing responsibilities. But he'd done his part financially, which enabled them to hire a nanny to supplement her mother's unpredictable schedule.

"Single parenthood definitely wasn't as prevalent as it is now. As a high school math teacher, I didn't make much money, so we had some lean times."

"Wasn't Aunt Mary a teacher too?"

Rose nodded. "For several years until she married. Her husband didn't want her to work."

"I only met him once. My mother isn't close to that side of her family. She never understood what Aunt Mary found so appealing about small-town living." Jillian recalled her mother's numerous derisive comments about her Southern ancestors. "As the years passed, their visits with one another grew fewer and farther between."

"As often happens, people grow apart." Sadness colored

Rose's words, but before Jillian could question it, Rose stood and began to stack their plates. "Would you like a slice of pie? Coffee?"

"That sounds great."

"It's a beautiful night. Why don't we take our dessert on the back porch and watch the sun set?"

Rose waved off Jillian's offer to wash the dishes, insisting she would do it later. So, instead, they settled on the porch, sipped coffee, and enjoyed fresh peach pie.

Jillian stared at the night sky and wondered whether she could see this many stars in Cincinnati, or if she'd just never bothered to look. Though the days were warm and humid, the nights were still cool and the air felt crisp. Crickets had replaced thc sounds of the city. Normally a driven person, Jillian wouldn't have thought she could enjoy sitting still so much. She couldn't remember the last time she'd spent an entire evening socializing. When she didn't skip her meals altogether, she either combined them with client meetings or ate on the run. She hoarded what little free time she did have, often taking a quick jog through her neighborhood to clear her head. But the pace of life was slower in Redmond. Maybe she should embrace the opportunity to relax, because she wouldn't have that chance when she returned home.

❖

"Andy, bring me some more water, will you?" Wil passed her Nalgene bottle over her shoulder.

"Sure thing, boss." Andy squeezed Wil's shoulder and bounded down the stairs toward a large orange cooler of water on the open tailgate of Wil's truck.

Andy had been on Wil's crew the longest of the three women. In fact, they had gone to high school together, though they hadn't hung out with each other then. Andy was the star player on the basketball team and had run with the popular crowd. When a knee injury blew her college scholarship, she had applied for work with Johnson and Son. Wil had been heading a crew of men at the time, and Bud had assigned Andy to work with her. Since then, as each of the men left the company, a woman had replaced him, at Wil's request. She preferred not to deal with the egos of men who didn't want to work for a woman.

They'd spent their first morning at Jillian's removing the appliances and starting to tear out the countertops and cabinets. Now they scattered across Jillian's front porch with their lunches spread out in front of them. Wil sat on the top step with her back pressed against the railing and her legs stretched out in front of her.

A few feet away, Andy's cousin, Tracy, sat cross-legged in the shade. The two women looked alike, with dark hair and skin, but their resemblance ended there. Andy's brown eyes were warm and friendly, whereas Tracy's, a shade deeper, were usually shadowed and secretive. Six months ago, when they'd lost a member of their crew, Wil had hired Tracy as a favor to Andy, but Tracy's quiet nature made her hard to get to know. Over time, Tracy had begun to open up, even smiling once in a while. Her grin transformed her face, lighting up her features and bringing out matching dimples.

Andy's partner, Patti, sat on the bottom step mirroring Wil's position. Patti was knowledgeable and hardworking, but most of all, her patience tempered Andy's excitable nature.

Andy stepped over Wil's legs and settled on the floor between them.

"Jillian Sealy sure is hot," Andy said as she unwrapped her sandwich. Patti gave her a sharp look. "What? You know you have my heart, but, come on, she is. I wonder what her deal is."

Wil ignored her, pretending to be engrossed in her potato chips.

"Wil, what do you think?"

"Huh?" Wil stalled.

"What do you know about Jillian?"

"Nothing, really." Wil and Andy had been friends for a long time, ever since they mutually decided they were incompatible as a couple. She knew Andy better than anyone else, which was probably why she hesitated to talk about Jillian. Andy loved good gossip, even when she herself was involved. It had taken only a day for word of Wil and Andy's split to spread around town. And Wil didn't want what had transpired between her and Jillian taking the same route.

"Come on, Wil. I heard you've been over to Rose Beam's with her and down to the hardware store. What did you two talk about?"

"About her plans for the house." Wil let her displeasure with Andy's prying seep into her voice.

"Andy, leave her alone," Patti warned, but Andy persisted.

"But is she a lesbian? Single?"

Wil balled her napkin and shoved it into her lunch bag. She stood and scowled down at Andy. "How about less talking and more eating, so we can get back to work." Wil strode down the steps toward her truck before Andy could respond, and she couldn't hear what she muttered to Patti.

Wil had just stowed her empty bag in her truck when she spotted Jillian walking up the sidewalk toward her. She slipped her sunglasses from her pocket and put them on before allowing her eyes to roam the length of Jillian's body. Pressed khaki slacks covered her long legs, but they would feel lean and strong wrapped around Wil. A sudden breeze molded Jillian's light cotton blouse to her torso, and the sensation of her breasts seemed to be burned into Wil's palms. She curled her fingers into fists and deliberately tried to replace her awareness with indifference.

"Did you have a nice walk?" Already losing her fight, she stepped closer.

"Yes. I met Rose at the diner for lunch."

Wil shook her head. "I don't know how you can eat there every day."

Jillian laughed and patted her stomach. "I'm going to gain thirty pounds before the house is ready."

"Oh, now, I know better than to say something like that to a woman."

"You didn't have to say it. I did." Jillian had never been a creature of habit, but the familiar faces and the heavy cooking smells as she walked in the diner were oddly comforting. She glanced toward the house. "Are you making progress?"

"Yeah. We're on track. What are you going to do this afternoon?" Wil raised her hand as if she wanted to touch Jillian's arm, then let it drop back to her side.

Suddenly, the only thing Jillian wanted to do was spend more time with Wil. "I don't know. What are you guys doing? Do you need any help?"

Wil gave a halfhearted smile, and Jillian was irritated that the sunglasses prevented her from seeing if it changed her eyes. Jillian imagined that if she could see them they would still be arctic and emotionless. She wondered if she would be so bothered by that thought if she hadn't already seen them bright with desire.

"I agreed to let you work on your projects at the same time. But I can't let you work *with* us."

"Why not?"

"For starters, my father would have a fit. Besides, that's why you're paying us. By tomorrow we'll have the kitchen completely gutted. We'll spend the rest of the week pushing out that wall and installing the new window in the breakfast nook. Next week I'll give you one day if you want to paint before we install the new cabinets."

"That would be easier than painting around them." Jillian made a mental note to go back down to the hardware store and buy the paint and supplies. "Your crew seems great. I get the impression you're all close."

"Andy and I are—friends. And she and Patti are together. I don't know Tracy very well, but Andy says she's good people."

"A whole crew of lesbians?"

Wil shook her head. "Tracy's straight. Recently divorced." Wil glanced toward the porch where the girls were cleaning up the remains of their lunch. "We better get back to work."

Jillian stood on the sidewalk as Wil quickly took the steps to the front porch. As she approached the other women, she pulled a small notebook out of her pocket and flipped it open. Though Jillian could hear the low timbre of Wil's voice, she wasn't close enough to hear her words. But her attention was focused on Wil's long fingers as they gestured toward the paper. The women listened carefully and nodded in respectful agreement.

She'd already decided that Wil was competent and dedicated. And judging from her suggestions at the hardware store, she could complement Jillian's vision for the finished renovation. Jillian was glad she hadn't let a night's indiscretion interfere with their professional relationship.

❖

A generic country band competed with the din of conversation and laughter throughout the darkened interior of Rambles Ranch. But sitting at the bar with her back to the crowd, Wil ignored the noise. She swirled three swallows of amber liquid in her mug and thought she should probably just finish her beer and go home. Not in the mood for company, she'd avoided making eye contact with anyone but the bartender. The only reason she'd even come out was because she'd grown tired of restlessly prowling her house and replaying intimate moments with Jillian.

Her first full day of working at Jillian's hadn't been too bad. They'd made a lot of progress and Jillian had stayed out of their way. But though Wil wanted to ignore her, she was constantly aware of the sounds of Jillian working in another part of the house. And she didn't like the blaze of arousal when she caught sight of Jillian passing through the hallway adjacent to the kitchen. There was absolutely no logical reason why helping Tracy rip out the old countertop should make her wet from the memory of taking Jillian on that very surface.

"What's on your mind?"

"Nothing." Wil glanced up as Andy settled on the stool next to her.

"Come on. I know that look. You're thinking about something serious."

"No. It's definitely not serious." Wil drained her mug and set it back on the bar. "I'm surprised your woman let you out of the house tonight."

"You know she hates it when you call her that." Andy signaled the bartender, pointed at Wil's empty glass, and held up two fingers. "She knows I'm safe if I'm out with you."

"Oh, yeah? Why's that?"

"Because you haven't let a woman within ten feet of you in months."

"If you only knew," Wil murmured, too low for Andy to hear over the music. She flashed on the image of Jillian's face as she climaxed and felt an answering tightness in her stomach.

"It's not like you couldn't have anyone you want. Especially after you spent most of last month sweating your ass off up on the church roof in your cargos and a tight white tee."

"We were working. And it was hot," Wil protested. "Besides, you were up there with me, and I don't recall you wearing much more."

"Sure. But I'm taken. And"—she pinched the spot on her side she referred to as a love handle—"I don't have your rock-hard body."

"Shut up." Wil laughed and punched Andy's arm.

"So what's the problem? You're not still pining after me, are you?" The reference to their relationship was a testament to how far they'd come. The jokes hadn't been so easy in the first few months. But now that Andy was happily involved with someone else, they'd both put the past behind them and their easy camaraderie had returned.

Wil shrugged. "This town is so damn small. Everybody who's single has been with everybody else. It just feels a little incestuous."

"Yeah, we need some fresh meat around here." Andy grinned and lifted her glass. "What about Jillian Sealy? She's definitely got a fresh—"

"Andy," Wil warned.

"What?"

"We're working for her." It certainly wasn't the first time Wil had crossed a line physically with a client. But the few times she had, she'd kept it from her crew. And it had never been more than a mutual sharing of pleasure. She didn't discuss her personal life, especially not her childhood. But despite the differences between them, something about Jillian invited her to open up. Even when she accused Jillian of condescending to her, Wil desperately wanted to change her mind, to prove she was worthy.

"Okay. But you have to admit she's gorgeous." Andy took a sip of her beer, then shrugged. "She's probably a snob anyway."

"Why do you say that?"

"Well, look at the way she dresses, all proper and perfectly creased. And that BMW sure wasn't cheap."

Wil had accused Jillian of being exactly how Andy was now assessing her. But for some reason, hearing Andy say it bothered Wil. Sure, Jillian's wardrobe was designer, her car screamed money, and she had a swagger in her walk that said she was entitled to something. But Wil had touched her, had held her while she pled for more, then tumbled into orgasm. Wil couldn't forget the passion she had seen beneath her cool exterior. Jillian Sealy had another layer, and Wil wanted to see it again.

Chapter Six

Get ready to sweat, folks, because we're in for a hot, hot summer. Today we'll have record high temps...

Jillian flipped the radio dial in search of music and, finding only a few options among the static, finally settled on a country station. She rolled up the sleeves of her old button-down shirt, then picked up a can of paint and poured some into a tray.

Within minutes she was immersed in the monotonous action of painting. Brad Paisley's guitar didn't quite drown out the rhythmic wet sound of the roller against the wall. She'd been fairly productive the previous week, completing some of her smaller projects while Wil's crew worked in the kitchen. Though they saw each other in passing, by tacit agreement, they avoided being alone together.

But even with that distance, Jillian noticed far more about Wil than she wanted to. One day she'd wandered into the driveway while taking a break and found Wil there measuring the wood that would frame the new window. Wil's eyebrows drew together in concentration as she pulled a pencil from behind her ear and marked the cuts. When Wil glanced up, for a moment, Jillian had been the subject of that intense focus. Without thinking she'd offered Wil her water bottle. When Wil had stepped close to take it, she smelled like sweat and sawdust, and Jillian wondered why that should be such an arousing combination.

Now she had to remind herself why she should just hurry up and get the house done and sold, and move on. Certainly, in the beginning flirting with Wil had been a nice distraction, and the sex—God, the sex had been incredible. But then she'd hurt Wil's feelings, though Wil had hidden it under anger, and things had become complicated. When their interaction was no longer a fun flirtation, she saw no point in carrying on, because it wasn't as if she intended to move to rural Tennessee and set up housekeeping with Wil Johnson. Though her time there was a nice break from her life, she just wasn't a small-town girl. Nor could she imagine Wil flourishing in her world back in Cincinnati.

She forced Wil from her mind and concentrated instead on her plans for the house, plotting again the changes she still wanted to make. She'd checked some comps in the area and had worked out her projected asking price. After reviewing Wil's schedule, she'd also set a tentative date for an open house.

Two hours later, her arms ached, but she'd nearly finished the first coat. That weather guy hadn't been joking. She took off her shirt, leaving only a tank top, and wiped a towel over her neck and chest. It wasn't even noon yet and the room was already stifling. She opened the kitchen window and a breeze swept in, pushing out the chemical smell of the paint and cooling her damp skin.

Before she could linger for long, she prodded herself back to work. Wil had only given her the one day for painting before her crew reclaimed the kitchen. Jillian sighed as her thoughts circled back to Wil, and she put a bit more muscle behind the roller to stave off the distraction.

❖

"Andy, hand me that pipe wrench," Wil said over her shoulder and held her arm out behind her. The cool metal handle was pushed into her hand. "Thanks."

Wil suspected the house had once had the heavy porcelain fixtures of its era, but at some point, the master bath had undergone a renovation. A stock vanity sink and a fiberglass tub and shower shell had been installed, probably in an effort to save money. The changes Jillian wanted to make would bring back some of the classic styles and add a few new trends. So while Andy and Tracy removed the shower, Wil disconnected the pipes that supplied the sink.

"Are you having any problems with that?" When she received no response, she glanced over her shoulder and found she was now alone in the room.

The showerhead and knobs lay on the floor, but other than that, it appeared little progress had been made. Wil didn't have to look very far for the two women. As she stepped out of the room she found both Andy and Tracy standing in the hallway and peeking into the kitchen.

As Wil approached quietly, Andy gave a low whistle. "So much for prim and proper."

"What are you—" As Wil looked around the doorjamb, her brain ceased to function. Jillian stood with her back to them, paint roller in hand. Her cutoff denim shorts ended just below the curve of her ass, leaving long legs exposed all the way down to her bare feet. When she stretched to reach the upper part of the wall, her ribbed tank top pulled tight. The muscles in her calves bunched as she rose to her tiptoes, and Wil imagined tracing her fingers down them, then taking one of those perfectly shaped feet in her hands. Busy enjoying the view, Wil was slow to realize that Andy and Tracy still stood beside her.

"Aren't you two supposed to be taking out that shower?" Wil snapped.

Andy's eyes never left Jillian, so she didn't see Wil's glare. "Are you kidding? And miss this—" She looked at Wil and choked off her words. "Uh, yeah. We're going."

"You don't want Patti to catch you ogling Jillian, anyway," Tracy teased as they headed for the bathroom.

Wil waited until they were gone to enter the kitchen. Jillian hadn't noticed her yet, so Wil admired her a moment longer before clearing her throat loudly enough to be heard over the music.

"Oh, hey, Wil." Jillian crossed to the counter and turned down the radio. "How's the bathroom coming along?" Wil seemed dazed, and when several seconds went by with no answer, she thought she'd have to repeat herself.

"Don't you think you should put some clothes on?"

Jillian looked down at herself, thinking she was sufficiently covered. "There's nothing wrong with what I'm wearing."

"You've got workers in the house."

Jillian was confused. She didn't think Wil was a prude, so what was the problem if she wanted to be comfortable in her own house? Just then one of Wil's crew passed the doorway, and when Jillian caught an appreciative glance, she thought she understood. She took a step closer, and Wil's eyes narrowed and she drew a quick breath. Jillian wanted to trace a fingertip along the neckline of Wil's T-shirt just to see what kind of reaction she would get. A thrill raced along her spine, but she didn't move, fearful that touching Wil would test her own willpower a bit too much.

"I have a house full of women, Wil. It's not like I have anything they haven't seen before."

"So if I had a man on my crew you would cover up?"

Jillian shrugged. "You don't."

"Andy's gay," Wil blurted almost desperately.

"I know. You told me. She and Patti seem pretty serious." Jillian could tell by Wil's expression that she realized it was a ridiculous thing to say. Despite her growing irritation, Jillian kept her tone even. She'd often found that the appearance of disinterest was as effective as raising her voice. And it was clear Wil was becoming frustrated with her lack of emotion.

"So you walking around half naked—"

"I am not half naked. You're overreacting. I was trying to let it go, but if you really want to force the issue, why does my attire have you so—bothered?"

"I'm not," Wil stuttered, and took a step back.

"Really? Because you seem a bit off-kilter."

"No. I'm perfectly—on-kilter."

Jillian smiled. "I don't think that's a word."

"If you want to walk around flaunting yourself, that's your business."

Wil still seemed flustered, and Jillian suspected she knew why, because her own awareness simmered just beneath her skin. They could probably go back and forth like this all day, when in truth they would both just get more and more aroused. She'd already endured waking after more than one erotic dream about Wil, so she was only torturing herself. But for reasons she didn't understand, Jillian couldn't back down.

Instead, she tossed her head deliberately and said, "I'm a single woman. Is there any reason why I shouldn't flaunt whatever I want to?"

Wil's jaw was tight as she stared at Jillian, then without

a word she turned and strode away, barely pausing as she met Andy in the living room.

"I'll be working at Miss Beam's. Call my cell if you need anything."

She was out the front door before Andy could reply. When Andy shrugged and headed for the bathroom, Jillian still stood watching through the screen door as Wil stalked to her truck. Wil was sexy when she was agitated. And since Jillian had already had a taste of that passion, she thought she might reconsider having a casual affair.

❖

Using the claw of her hammer, Wil pried plank after plank from the deck of Rose's porch. The destructive activity was just what she needed. She'd arrived still steaming from her encounter with Jillian and had stopped only long enough to tell Rose she was there before she got to work. She was wound up, and since releasing that tension with Jillian the way she really wanted to was out of the question, she'd do it here, tearing away the rotted boards.

She didn't know why Jillian got so far under her skin, but it seemed anytime she was around, Wil was either turned on or irritated. Sure, she'd had relationships, some serious and some—well, not so serious. She certainly wasn't a prude, and in her younger days she'd had no aversion to physical interactions with no future. But she wasn't a kid anymore. Now she wanted more.

She saw what Andy and Patti had and she wanted that—someone to share her life with, someone to build that house with, another person who knew her completely. And it was clear Jillian Sealy wasn't that woman. Her time in Redmond was far too temporary. Wil could almost feel the days ticking away. She couldn't explain it, but somehow she knew that she'd never be able to keep things strictly physical between them even for the short weeks until Jillian left. Since she wasn't up for having her heart broken, it was best to keep her distance, which was frustrating as hell when she kept remembering how it felt to touch her.

Yes, she'd overreacted to Jillian's attire, but after she'd opened her mouth she couldn't figure out how to back down. So she'd latched on to a reason to leave. She *had* promised Rose she'd come over, and her crew had things covered at Mary's. Despite the legitimate excuse, Wil couldn't stop thinking about Jillian, and that bothered her. No one had ever gotten to her so much that she couldn't lose herself in her work. Since the day she'd hired on with her father, it had always been her escape from whatever weighed on her personally.

But now, at odd moments, the memory of Jillian's lilting laugh, of the way her smile lifted one side of her mouth slightly more than the other, or of the unexpected contrast of solid metal against Jillian's tender nipple distracted her. Jesus, it was that kind of thinking that would get her in trouble. But despite knowing this, she involuntarily recalled the feel of that nipple against her tongue.

Just as her mind took hold of that image, Rose came around the corner of the house, and Wil shifted gears.

"I hope being here isn't keeping you from anything important at Mary's." In one hand Rose carried a pair of gardening gloves, and in the other a small foam pad meant for kneeling next to flower beds.

"Oh, no, ma'am. Andy, Tracy, and Patti are taking care of things." Wil paused and laid down her hammer. "Jillian's painting the kitchen today."

"She's a sweet girl."

Wil could think of several other adjectives for Jillian, such as stubborn, spoiled, smart, and sexy.

"She's got backbone and a mind of her own too. She reminds me of Mary when we were just a bit younger than she is now." Rose smiled. "Do you think Mary knew Jillian was so much like her?"

"I doubt it. I got the impression that Jillian didn't know Mary well at all. Still, there must be a reason Mary chose her."

"I'm sure there was." For a moment, Wil thought she was going to say more, but she changed the subject. "I have bingo, then lunch with the ladies tomorrow. But I never lock the back door, so if you come over, just go on in the house."

Wil nodded and picked up her hammer. Even though things were changing all over the world, it was still safe to leave the door unlocked in Redmond.

The small town had a sense of history that had dissipated in America's cities. In Redmond, everyone knew everyone else, and folks could still tell stories about someone's ancestors. Where else would so many people remember when Boone Rivers got arrested for painting "Marry me, Becky" on the side of her daddy's barn? Her father had dropped the charges, but only after Boone had repainted the entire barn. Of course, Wil suspected Becky's father didn't still have any hard feelings, since Becky and Boone had just given him his fifth grandchild.

CHAPTER SEVEN

The edge of the island will start here." Wil pulled a tape measure to a point near the center of the kitchen.

"How long is it?" Patti knelt beside her.

"Six feet," Wil recalled quickly, without looking at her notes.

She had been back to Jillian's only briefly in the two days since they'd argued, and had purposely stopped by to check the progress when she knew Jillian was out. Her crew was installing the new floor in the kitchen, and she really didn't need to supervise such a simple task. Instead, she'd finished the projects at Rose's.

But the cabinets were being delivered today, so she'd had to return. When she'd walked into the kitchen moments ago, Jillian had been talking with Patti and Tracy. But Wil needn't have worried if she should apologize to Jillian, because just then Jillian's cell rang and she excused herself to answer it.

So, while they waited, Wil began to go over the layout of the new kitchen with her crew. She paced out the dimensions she and Jillian had discussed, pleased with the traffic flow in the new area. She imagined how easily anyone could move from the refrigerator to the stove or island while preparing meals.

"It's going to be a beautiful kitchen. Did Jillian design it?" Patti asked as Wil indicated where the dishwasher would go.

"She had the initial plans and I altered them a bit."

"Well, it's great. You work well together." When Wil didn't respond she continued, "What's going on between you two?"

Wil glanced up sharply. "I thought meddling was your wife's job."

"Hey," Andy protested.

But Patti shrugged, unperturbed. "Usually. But I'll make an exception for you."

"Don't." She didn't want to talk about Jillian, least of all in front of her entire crew. Patti was crossing a line in their normal working relationship.

Patti ignored her warning. "One of the things I've enjoyed about working with you all these years is how easygoing you are. I've never seen you spend so much time away from a job—"

"You guys have handled things just fine without me."

"And when you are around you're jumpy as hell." Patti went on as if Wil hadn't spoken. "You bristle every time anyone even mentions Jillian's name."

"Damn it, Patti. I said drop it." When a horn sounded outside, Wil seized the reason to escape. "We have more important things to do than stand around analyzing my moods."

She walked out through the garage as a white box truck lumbered to a stop at the curb and Bill leaned out the open window.

"Got a delivery for you," he called as she came down the driveway.

"Hang on. I'll get Jillian to move her car and you can back in here," Wil said before jogging back to the house.

Jillian was pacing the backyard, still on the phone. Wil paused as she stepped onto the back porch, and Jillian stopped with her back to Wil and threw up one hand.

"I'm working on it, Mom. Doing it right takes time. Yes, I'll be there." Obviously frustrated, she spun around and saw Wil standing there. "I've gotta go. I'll call you later."

"Sorry. Bill's here and we need you to move your car."

"My mother," Jillian explained unnecessarily as she flipped the phone shut. "Reminding me that their anniversary party is the day after tomorrow."

"Are you heading home, then?" Though she'd been avoiding Jillian, a hollow feeling still accompanied the thought of her leaving.

"Just for a couple days. She's in a hurry for me to get back home for good, though."

"If I recall, you were in a bit of a rush as well."

"I was. I mean, I still am." Jillian paused, seeming to weigh her words. "But there's something about this house I don't want to let go of."

"It doesn't seem practical to keep it. There's not a lot of money in rental properties in this town."

"No, I can't imagine that there is." Jillian pulled her keys from her pocket and tossed them to Wil. "Move it wherever you need to."

Jillian watched her go, then resumed her pacing. Her conversation with her mother had left her agitated. But more than her mother's words, Jillian was unsettled by her own feelings. She had no connection to this home or the people who made their lives here. But she'd begun to feel invested on more than a financial level.

"This is ridiculous," she murmured. She had always been business-minded and her goals hadn't changed. Sell the house, get back to civilization, and find another job. She was surprised at how unconcerned she was with what direction her career would ultimately take. They must put something in the water here. Because certainly that was the only way she could be feeling misty about some small town, an aunt she never knew, and an old house. She purposely left Wil off that list.

❖

"Everything you ordered for the kitchen and master bath is here." Bill handed over a clipboard with the invoice attached for Wil to sign.

When he tore off the yellow copy of the invoice and handed it to her, Wil scanned it, but the prices were higher than she expected. They'd carried the cabinets into the dining room and stacked the rest of the boxes in the garage. She crossed to a nearby box, flicked open her pocket knife, and sliced through the tape. She examined the kitchen faucet, then one of the bathroom ones as well.

"Bill, these aren't the faucets I ordered."

"I know. Miss Jillian was in last week and changed the order."

"But these cost twice as much as the ones we originally chose."

He shrugged. "I told her how much they were."

"Damn it," Wil mumbled.

"Do you want me to send them back?"

Wil considered it, thinking that since Jillian didn't consult her before changing the order, she shouldn't have to check with her either. But then Jillian would probably insist on the more expensive ones anyway, so she decided they might as well have this fight now rather than when the original fixtures came in. "No. I'll take them for now. But if I talk her into the cheaper ones, can I return them?"

"Sure thing, Wil." His exprcssion said he doubted she'd change Jillian's mind, and Wil was afraid he was right. He shook her hand, then climbed into the cab of his truck.

When Wil walked into the dining room, Jillian was admiring the cabinets as Andy, Patti, and Tracy removed the protective packing.

"I can't wait to see these installed. Do we have the countertop too?" She looked around.

"It's over here." Tracy crossed to several long expanses of granite leaned against the far wall. She smiled shyly at Jillian and peeled back the corner of the protective paper, revealing the dark marbled surface. "This stuff is so durable. Once we get it sealed it won't scratch, chip, or stain."

Wil stared, thinking that was the most she'd heard Tracy say to Jillian at once.

Jillian moved to Tracy's side and examined the countertop. "It'll look great." When Jillian gave her an excited smile, Tracy blushed.

"The faucets and fixtures are in the garage, if you'd like to see them as well," Wil said quietly.

Judging from Jillian's guilty expression, she knew right away what was wrong. "Wil, I—"

"Come look at them." Wil took Jillian's arm and led her toward the garage. She didn't want to argue in front of her crew.

"Hey," Jillian protested as Wil practically shoved her through the door. She jerked her arm out of Wil's grasp. "I don't think that was necessary."

Normally, Wil wouldn't touch a client, but considering how familiar they'd been, she hadn't given it a second thought. She reached into the open box, pulled out a kitchen faucet, and held it in front of Jillian. "Do you want to tell me what this is?"

"Well, if you don't know, then I've hired the wrong contractor," Jillian shot back sarcastically.

"I'm serious, Jillian."

"What's the problem? I can afford it."

"Well, for starters, you could have told me so I didn't look like an idiot with Bill. I should know what orders are going through for my job site."

"You would've tried to talk me out of it."

"Damn right. If you keep making expensive choices you're cutting into your profit. These faucets aren't going to raise the value of the house."

"I know." Jillian sighed. Wil was giving her the same advice she would give a client. But she hadn't considered that when she'd changed the order. She couldn't seem to stop imagining how she would decorate the house if she were keeping it. "But I was down there getting the paint and when I saw these, I just had to have them."

"I can return them and get the less expensive ones. It won't delay our timeline if we just move on and install them when they come in." Wil began to put them back in the box, but Jillian stopped her with a hand on her arm.

"No. They're here now. I'd like to keep them." She'd made a decision, and Wil's assumption that she would abandon it at the first challenge only hardened her resolve.

"It's not a smart investment."

"I know."

"You've got to be the most stubborn—" Realizing she was raising her voice, Wil paused and took a breath. She didn't want her crew to overhear them arguing. "Jillian, what am I missing?" Initially, Wil had gotten the impression that Jillian was smart and ambitious about making money on the sale of Mary's house. Now she seemed not only to be hesitant, but also recklessly spending money in ways that wouldn't benefit her in the long run. "I thought I understood your goals for this project."

"I thought I did too." Jillian pulled a key from her pocket and handed it to Wil. "I've got to do this anniversary thing. I'm going to leave early in the morning and drive up. Will you take care of things here while I'm gone? Please, don't forget to lock up when you're not here."

"What?" The quick subject change confused Wil. Jillian had asserted her opinion and now she was refusing to discuss it further. But Wil was not so easily distracted. "We're not done talking about this."

"Yes. We are. Put in the fixtures I ordered."

Wil wanted to argue, but her father's philosophy regarding pleasing the client echoed in her head. Besides, what business was it of hers if this particular client wanted to waste her money? So instead, she inclined her head in mock submission. "The customer is always right."

Jillian smiled. "See that you remember that."

"I will. Do you have any other decrees?" Wil was quite aware that when it came to Jillian, she gave in more than she normally would. And that thought made her uncomfortable, but she couldn't ignore Jillian's mildly flirtatious tone.

Jillian's smile widened. "I might be able to think of something. So long as you remember who's the boss."

Pleasure curled tightly in Wil's stomach. Jillian's words should have reminded her that she would always be someone's underling. From anyone else they would have inspired anger. But somehow the thought of Jillian controlling her in an entirely different way brought a surprisingly strong wave of arousal. Suddenly she was glad Jillian would be gone for a few days, because distance was exactly what she needed.

❖

"Wil, it's almost eight o'clock. How late do you plan to work?"

Wil craned her head to look out from the cabinet under the sink where she was installing the plumbing. Andy stood bent over with a plaintive look on her face but Wil wasn't swayed. "Until it's done. Stop whining."

Andy had already asked three times in the last two hours if they could go home, and she was getting on Wil's nerves. All of a sudden her crew was averse to a little hard work?

"I'm not whining. You're a damn slave driver."

"We're not getting any closer to done with you just standing around." Wil scooted out and stood up to face her.

"There's at least two hours of work left here. Just because you don't have a life, that doesn't mean the rest of us don't have things to do." Andy planted her hands on her hips, and Wil knew she was bracing for a showdown.

Patti said diplomatically, "We *have* been working late every day. Maybe we could just get a fresh start Monday."

"Jillian's going to be back tomorrow and I want this done before then."

"So we all have to suffer so you can impress a woman you're never going to make a move on anyway?"

"Andy, hold on," Tracy began, but Andy cut her off.

"No." She turned challenging eyes on Wil. "Do you think we don't see the way you stare at her? Yeah, she's good-looking. But please don't make a fool of yourself. She's leaving in a couple of weeks, and she won't give this place a second thought."

"Wait a damn minute. A few weeks ago you were trying to convince me to go after her. But now I'm making a fool of myself?"

"Wil, we just don't want you to get hurt." Patti stepped between them and put a hand on her shoulder.

Wil glanced at each of them, seeing sympathy in three pairs of eyes, and realized they'd come to a consensus before this conversation. "So you've all been discussing this. Sitting around talking about how pathetic Wil is for chasing some chick that's out of her league."

"If anyone thinks she's out of your league, it's her," Andy shot back angrily.

"She's not like that."

"She knows she's hot and thinks you should just fall at her feet and—"

"She's not like that," Wil repeated firmly, uncertain if she was trying to convince Andy or herself. She watched Andy's eyes narrow with comprehension.

"You slept with her."

"What?"

"Are you crazy?"

Patti and Tracy spoke at the same time, protesting, then fell silent when Wil didn't argue.

All three women stared at her until Andy broke the silence. "How was it?"

"Amazing," Wil answered honestly.

"I can't believe I didn't see it before now. How long has this been going on?" Andy asked, and Wil knew she was hurt that she hadn't told her.

"It happened once. Two weeks ago."

"So what now?"

Wil shook her head. "Nothing."

"Why not?"

"You said it yourself. She's leaving in a couple of weeks."

"But if you—"

"It's late. Let's call it a night. In fact, take the rest of the weekend." Wil made it clear she didn't want to discuss Jillian further. "Try to keep this to yourself, please, Andy, at least until she leaves." She wasn't worried about her own reputation, but she didn't want to take a chance Jillian might find out people were gossiping about her.

"Don't worry, Wil. She'll keep her mouth shut," Patti assured her, giving Andy a stern look. "Let's go, girls."

They quickly packed up and headed for the front door. The last of the three to leave, Patti paused and looked back. "You coming, Wil?"

"Yeah. I'm going to clean up a little, then lock up."

Patti nodded, then, apparently not fooled, she said, "Don't work too late."

When they'd gone, Wil crawled back under the sink. She hadn't wanted her crew to find out that she'd been with Jillian and hoped one of them wouldn't slip up and say something in front of Jillian. After she'd finished the plumbing, she installed the faucet.

Despite Patti's admonishment, Wil worked well into the night. She thought briefly about going down to Rambles Ranch. Friday nights were usually busy, and she could probably find someone to take her mind off Jillian Sealy. But in a moment of honesty she admitted that probably wasn't going to happen.

Though she knew it was foolish, as if she were a teenager trying to impress a crush, she wanted to present Jillian the finished kitchen when she returned the next afternoon. When she was a teen she'd never had the means or the confidence to impress anyone. An outsider, confused about her own identity, Wil wasn't sought after by any of the boys in her class. And even if she'd admitted to herself she was attracted to girls, she wouldn't have been brave enough to act on her feelings.

But after high school, she'd outgrown her concern about anyone else's opinion. The business was doing well and she'd bought her house. Finally, she began to feel like she had something to offer. And once she'd accepted her homosexuality, she'd discovered that the same qualities that made her unattractive to the boys made the women want her.

CHAPTER EIGHT

Jillian stepped out of her BMW and shaded her eyes against the late-afternoon sun hanging low in the sky. Wil sat on the front porch of Mary's house, elbows resting on her knees. As she popped the trunk, Wil stood. Dressed completely in black, she looked lean, dangerous, and exciting. And though Jillian was exhausted after the nine-hour drive from Ohio, she couldn't think of anything she'd rather come home to. Except this wasn't home, and Wil wasn't hers.

"Welcome back." Wil joined her next to the car. "Did you have a nice trip?"

"Two days with my entire family," Jillian answered sarcastically, pulling her suitcase and laptop bag from her trunk. "It was a laugh a minute."

"Not close to your folks?"

"Actually, I am. But they maintain a level of pretense that can be exhausting."

Jillian had always known that about her parents, but it had never been so obvious as these past couple of days. When she'd told her mother about her work on Mary's house, she'd received only a condescending look and a snippy comment about working among rednecks rubbing off on her. Her father hadn't reacted much better, saying that she should sell the house under market value and get back home. He warned she was wasting her time. But as she thought about how much more relaxed and stress-free life felt there, she didn't think it was a waste. And she still believed she would make more profit on the house after the work was done. But she'd have to decide soon about whether to continue the renovation.

She'd gone by her condo to check on things and retrieved a voice mail from her former firm's biggest competitor. The president had called her personally, kissing ass on her answering machine and imploring her to return his call so they could discuss a "mutually beneficial proposal." She'd let him wait one more day before phoning him back and he'd offered her a top spot at his firm, but he wanted her there next week. She'd asked for two more weeks, claiming she still had matters in her aunt's estate to wrap up.

Wil picked up Jillian's suitcase and followed her toward the house. "Do you have any siblings?"

"One brother. He and his wife have four boys."

"Wow. I'll bet that's a handful."

"They kept hoping for a girl. His wife would give it one more try, if he'd agree. But I think he's done."

"I can't imagine such a big family. It's just been me and my dad for so long." Wil held the front door open.

"Do you see your mother often?" Jillian dropped her luggage right inside.

"More than I used to. When she first left, I was angry and didn't want to have anything to do with her. Plus, Dad needed me. We had a rough time for a while."

"And now?"

"Now I'm trying to understand that it wasn't really about us, because we couldn't make her happy. She had to do that for herself."

Jillian was curious about how the emotionally injured

child Wil described had grown into the strong woman standing before her.

"So you've lived here all your life?"

"Born and raised."

"Have you ever thought about living anyplace else?"

"You mean, anyplace *bigger*?" Defensiveness colored her tone.

"Well, yes." Jillian refused to apologize for believing there was more out there than this small town could offer.

"I'm not sheltered. I've visited other places, but I'll always come back here. This is home."

"But there's so much more to the world than Redmond." Even after Jillian's time here, she could only begin to imagine the differences in their childhoods. Certainly, Wil's father had never taken her to the theater or the symphony. Jillian had grown up being shuttled from ballet lessons to soccer practice by the current nanny. In high school, she'd excelled at academics, but her priority had been making sure she kept up with the latest fashion trends so as not to be outdone by a classmate.

"I have everything I need here." Wil's answer was quick, as if she couldn't miss what she'd never had. She took Jillian's hand and led her toward the kitchen. "Come see what we did while you were gone."

What Jillian saw as they stepped in the room far surpassed her vision. The pristine cabinets contrasted beautifully with the dark countertop and tile floor. Natural light washed in through the new, larger window, making the room feel airy and open. The appliances had come in while she was gone, and seeing their sleek exteriors fall in perfectly with the design of the room made Jillian wish she knew how to cook.

"Oh, Wil, it's perfect." She squeezed Wil's hand, not having realized until then that she still held it.

"If kitchens really do sell houses, you shouldn't have any problem unloading this one."

"Yeah." Jillian released Wil's hand and wandered around the room, touching surfaces and opening drawers. "I guess I'll go get some things, so at least I can make coffee and a few simple meals."

"So, peanut butter and jelly, then?" Wil said.

Jillian smiled. "That sounds about right." She ran a hand along the edge of the sink.

"We still have some minor touches." Wil watched as Jillian tested the faucet, then when their eyes met, she said, "Yes. It looks good. But I still say you should have stuck with the less expensive ones."

Jillian raised an eyebrow and laughed. "Can't just admit I was right, can you?"

Wil shrugged. "It's your money." The new faucet complemented the kitchen design perfectly, and Wil might have chosen it herself if it were for her own home. But she wouldn't tell Jillian that.

"You guys must have worked hard to get all this done."

"Once we got started, everything went smoothly."

❖

Jillian opened her eyes and the sun slashing through the window sent a blinding pain through her skull. Trying to escape, she rolled over, but her stomach violently protested the sudden movement and a deep throb began in her temple.

"Oh shit," she muttered. "I cannot be sick." Keeping her eyes tightly closed, she groped for the cordless phone on the nightstand, then dialed by feel.

She told Rose she wouldn't be able to make it to Sunday brunch as they'd planned. After disconnecting the phone, she dropped it on the floor beside the bed, drew her knees up to her chest, and concentrated very hard on not moving at all.

She must have fallen asleep because the next time she opened her eyes, the sun had stretched farther across the bed. Tentatively, she stretched out, then sat up slowly. Her nausea seemed to have lessened and the throbbing behind her eyes had eased, but her sinuses still felt as if they were stuffed with cotton. Maybe a cup of tea would help.

She was on her way to the kitchen when the doorbell rang. Flinching at the loud peal, she detoured to the front door, intent on getting there before her visitor felt the need to ring again.

She swung open the door just as Wil reached for the button.

"Don't touch it," she said softly, and Wil jerked her arm back. "What are you doing here?" Wil usually gave her crew Sundays off. Through the fog in her head, Jillian tried to recall if she'd mentioned that they would be working today.

She folded her arms over her chest, suddenly conscious of the fact that she had on her most worn pair of flannel pajama pants and a thin T-shirt, and she hadn't showered since yesterday. Wil, on the other hand, looked great, dressed casually in khaki shorts and a navy V-neck shirt. She carried a paper bag and a large Tupperware bowl.

"Rose said you were sick," Wil said, as if that explained everything. Without waiting for an invitation, she slipped past Jillian and headed for the kitchen. "I made you some soup."

"Soup?" Jillian echoed. Still confused, she turned and followed Wil. "I have soup. There's a can of chicken noodle in the pantry."

"Canned soup? No." Wil abandoned the crackers and ginger ale she'd unpacked and steered Jillian toward the living room. "You need homemade soup."

"I don't know what all the fuss is about, it's just a cold."

Jillian sat and allowed Wil to drape the throw from the back of the sofa around her shoulders.

Wil touched Jillian's forehead and she leaned into the touch. Wil's hand felt cool against her feverish skin. "It's more than just a cold. Now, be a good girl and lay down while I heat this up." Wil gripped her shoulders and guided her gently back.

When she seemed satisfied Jillian would stay on the sofa, she disappeared into the kitchen once again. Jillian shivered and pulled the blanket tighter around her. From the sounds of Wil moving around the kitchen, she could picture the activity taking place there. Wil pulled a pot from the cabinet and placed it on the stove with a series of metallic clangs, then ice cubes clinked into a glass.

Closing her aching eyes, Jillian allowed the sounds to drift in her head. She slid into the comforting cocoon and stopped fighting the exhaustion that swept over her.

❖

"Soup's read—"

Wil strode into the living room and pulled up short as she saw Jillian lying on the couch with her forearm flung across her face. She'd tossed off the blanket and it now lay on the floor. Wanting to let her rest, Wil began to back out of the room.

"I'm not sleeping," Jillian croaked. She opened her eyes and shoved herself into a sitting position.

Mindful of the bowl she carried, Wil settled on the sofa next to her and handed it to her. "Be careful, it's still hot."

Jillian took a tentative spoonful. "It's good. Thank you."

"Homemade chicken soup is always the cure." Wil picked up the blanket and tucked it around Jillian again.

"Why are you being so nice to me?"

Wil shrugged. "You don't have any family here. People should be cared for when they're sick."

Jillian had never needed a caretaker; she was very self-sufficient. But she enjoyed Wil's attention. Since she couldn't tell Wil that, she opted for a joke. "That damned Southern hospitality again."

Wil flushed and looked away. "I'm sorry. I'll go."

As Wil stood, Jillian grabbed her wrist. "*I'm* sorry. I didn't mean to sound ungrateful. I'm just not used to strangers being nice."

Wil glanced at Jillian's hand. "Well, we're not really strangers, are we?"

Wil's skin felt hot beneath her fingers and Jillian released her. "No, I guess we're not."

"Jillian, I—"

"I'd like it if you would keep me company for a while." Jillian didn't want to hear whatever Wil had been about to say. The embarrassment hadn't fully faded from her eyes and Jillian felt guilty for putting it there. She hadn't meant to insult Wil's generosity. She'd just been uncomfortable with the tenderness Wil had shown her. From the first day they'd met, she'd been willing to acknowledge the physical pull between them, but today their connection had another layer. And the more she learned about Wil, the more she felt as if she'd underestimated her depth.

Wil nodded, sat back down, and waited patiently while she consumed the soup. Jillian hadn't had an appetite all day, but the flavorful broth soothed her and she finished as much as she could before setting the bowl on the coffee table.

"The soup really was thoughtful." Jillian yawned. "I'm sorry. I can't seem to stay awake for long today."

"I'd hate to think I'm boring."

"Certainly not."

"Good. Come here." Wil pulled a pillow onto her lap. She coaxed Jillian to lie down, then stroked her hair off her forehead.

Jillian rested her cheek against Wil's stomach and wrapped her arms around herself. She looked up at Wil and wondered how she'd come to feel so comfortable with her. From the moment they'd met, Jillian hadn't been herself. Anyone who knew her would be shocked by the fact that she'd slept with Wil the second time she'd seen her. Not normally a physical person, Jillian found herself constantly inventing reasons to touch Wil, even casually. Now here she was letting Wil see her at her absolute worst. But it didn't matter because Wil had taken care of her, made her feel secure, and though her head still throbbed, she felt better.

Just then, she didn't want to leave Redmond. But she needed to eventually—maybe sooner than she'd planned.

"I got a call from a competing firm," Jillian said. Her sluggish mind muddled through the offer again, but she knew she wasn't in any shape to make a decision.

Wil's fingers paused in her hair. "And?"

"He made me an offer I shouldn't refuse."

"Don't you mean *can't* refuse?"

"No. Shouldn't." It was a sweet deal. Only two weeks ago, the thought of going back to Cincinnati and helping them surpass her former employer would have inspired her bloodlust. Maybe when she was feeling better, thinking clearly, she wouldn't dread taking the job. "It's conditional. He wants me to start in three weeks." She chuckled. "I think he's afraid if he doesn't get me signed on quickly, someone will make me a better offer."

"Is it a good firm?"

"They've got a great reputation and are doing a lot of high-dollar development deals. There's potential for me to make a ton of money."

"Sounds like a perfect fit for you."

"It is." Jillian nodded slowly. *Or it would have been two weeks ago.*

"I thought you were tired?" Concern darkened Wil's eyes to the color of new denim.

Jillian reached up and traced Wil's jaw. "I am."

"So, sleep." Wil's fingers skated over Jillian's brow, then she caught Jillian's hand and held it.

Turning on her side, Jillian cradled their joined hands against her chest and closed her eyes. "You'll stay?" she murmured, though she was too drowsy to wait for Wil's response.

❖

"I need to pull your crew off the Sealy job." Wil's father didn't wait for her to get settled in the chair across the desk from him before he broke the bad news.

"For how long?" She sat slowly, not panicking. It wasn't unheard of for a crew to be shifted for a day or two to help finish another project. Then if they kicked things up a notch, they could easily make up any time lost at Jillian's.

"A couple of weeks. Three at the most. Alton's crew isn't going to have the school renovation done in time. I need you to go over there and help them catch it up." He twirled a pen in his fingers and with the other hand flipped through a stack of papers.

"You've got be kidding." Now she was panicking. "We're on schedule. Jillian's going to be pissed."

"We'll have to give her a break on her rate or something. The school is one of our biggest accounts, and it's got to be done before the new school year starts up."

"Dad, this just looks bad." She understood the need to complete the school project. But they'd made a commitment to Jillian's job, and Wil's mind raced for a solution that would allow her to honor it.

Her father sighed and threw the pen down on the desk in front of him. "I know. We're overextended and this one got away from me. I'm going to have to do something about those lazy college boys on Alton's crew. But for now we need to clean up their mess."

"Let's split my crew. I'll send Tracy and Patti to the school. If we work our butts off, Andy and I can keep Jillian's on schedule." Wil didn't even want to think about telling Jillian they'd be off her job for a few weeks.

Their truce had been tentative at best, and Wil readily admitted it was her fault. But she was still shaken by the feelings caring for Jillian while she was ill had stirred. And she couldn't stop replaying Jillian's drowsy declaration that she'd been offered another job and now dreaded the day Jillian would tell her she had accepted the job and was leaving. Wil had never felt the aching tenderness that had swept over her while Jillian had rested with her head pillowed in Wil's lap. She had fled as soon as she was certain Jillian was sleeping deeply enough not to notice. In the three days since then, they'd gone back to polite reserve while Wil tried to convince herself that nothing had changed.

Bud seemed to be considering her proposal, but he shook his head. "Three of you need to go to the school. Either you or Andy can stay on at Miss Sealy's. That's the best I can do."

"There's no way one of us can get everything done."

"I'm sorry, Wil. But the job for the school district is

important. There's a rumor they're going to overhaul the county courthouse next year, and I'm hoping to get that job. But if we can't make this deadline we don't have a prayer."

"Dad—"

"It's done." He cut her protest off with a raised palm.

Jillian was going to be livid. One of them needed to stay and do what they could at Mary's in order to soften the blow, but she couldn't leave the task to Andy. The only way she would feel confident that the work was going as smoothly and quickly as possible was to do it herself. Besides, she needed to see Jillian. She'd go crazy working with Alton and thinking about Jillian.

"I'll send the three of them to the school in the morning," she said.

"Good. Tell them to report to Alton. Do you want me to call Miss Sealy and explain?"

"No. I'll tell her."

CHAPTER NINE

"Hey, Miss Sealy," Bill called from the doorway of the hardware store. He flipped the Open sign hanging in the window.

Jillian smiled and waved, but didn't detour from her path. Accustomed to waking early, she'd been taking regular walks around town, often setting out while the clouds were still painted pink. It hadn't rained in weeks and this morning promised another scorcher. The air was already warm and humid, and the sun hadn't even cut through the haze yet.

She passed the post office just as one of the carriers stepped outside with an overflowing mailbag slung over his shoulder. Next door a firefighter raised Old Glory on the flagpole in front of the fire station. Only a few other people walked along the sidewalk, none in a hurry to reach their destination. Jillian reached the corner and waited just a second for a car to pass, then crossed and turned north toward home.

The easy pace of this small town as it began gearing up for the day was so different from the driving rhythm of the city, with its congested traffic and the fast click of expensively shod feet on the sidewalks. Jillian certainly didn't miss being jostled along by a crowd as she made her way to her office.

The diner was already full of patrons eating breakfast and lingering over coffee. As Jillian passed it, her body clamored for caffeine but she kept her pace, knowing that by the time she got home a fresh pot would be brewing. As soon as the kitchen was functional, Wil had begun to make coffee when she arrived, and by the time Jillian returned from her walk the crew was ready to take a break and they all shared a cup together.

Since she'd been sick, they hadn't had much interaction aside from this morning ritual. After the compassion with which Wil had treated her that day, Jillian had expected more familiarity between them, but Wil seemed to prefer even more distance now. When her crew was around, she treated Jillian with impersonal respect. And the few times they'd been alone together, she'd acted as if she was in a hurry to get away. Soon taking the hint, and far too proud to try to change Wil's mind, Jillian had simply left the polite space between them.

As she turned the corner she heard the high-pitched whine of a saw, which got louder as she approached her garage. The overhead door was open and, inside, Wil leaned over a wet saw, carefully cutting a piece of tile. She paused and glanced up as Jillian passed.

"Good morning." Wil's stomach twisted with nervousness and she wondered how long she could put off revealing that she was down to a crew of one.

"Morning. Coffee ready?"

"Yep," Wil replied. Jillian was always somewhat single-minded after her walk.

Wil consulted her notes, then measured the next tile. She was about to turn the saw back on when Jillian reappeared and lounged in the doorway, cradling a mug in one hand.

"Where is everyone?"

Wil took off her safety glasses and set them on the makeshift table. “It’s just me today.”

“What happened?”

“Well, actually, it’s just me for a while. We’ve had a bit of an emergency on another job and I had to send the girls over there.”

“For how long?” Jillian tried not to panic, hoping it would be only a couple of days, and it wouldn’t affect her projected listing date.

“I don’t know. A few weeks maybe.”

“A few…” Jillian was completely at a loss. They were supposed to be finished in less than three weeks. “Which job was more important than mine?”

Wil winced. “The school.”

“Ah, I see. The hometown team gets priority,” Jillian said calmly. Considering Wil’s dedication, she knew if there was a better option Wil would have taken it, so there was no point in getting angry. As an idea formed, she realized she would need her energy elsewhere.

“There was nothing I could do.” Wil sounded truly apologetic.

“So, *now* you’ll let me work with you.”

“No.”

She planted a hand on her hip and gave Wil her hardest stare. “I’m sorry if that sounded like a question, because it wasn’t.”

“No. You’re not working with me. I’ll get it done.” Wil lifted her chin a notch and Jillian was actually impressed. Lesser men and women had backed down from her before.

“I’m sure you will. But *you* don’t need to. I want this done. Do you really expect me to sit around while you do it all?”

“Yes. That’s what you’re paying me for.”

Jillian carefully skirted the stacks of tile on the floor and stepped closer to Wil. "Stop thinking that you work for me." The resolve in Wil's eyes didn't waver, even when Jillian took her hand. "Circumstances have changed, and now we're in this together."

"I can't let you do it."

Jillian knew where Wil's resistance stemmed from and, hoping it would pay off, she bluffed. "Then I'll take my business elsewhere."

"No one else is going to do it faster. You'll have a hard time finding someone who can even start for a few weeks."

"I know. But as I'll tell your father, Johnson and Son has shown just how little my project means to them. And since you're not showing enough flexibility to consider my suggestion, I'd rather someone else take twice as long than keep you on the job." She saw the evidence of her barb in the quick tightening around Wil's eyes and didn't wait for a response. "Here's my plan. The exterior paint will take forever with just two of us. So I'll hire painters. Other than that, I think you and I can handle everything. I don't know much about all this sawing and measuring." She waved her hand toward the table behind Wil. "But I take direction well—I can bring you stuff, hold things while you hammer," she laughed, "basically do whatever grunt work you've got. It has to be better than working by yourself."

The corner of Wil's mouth twitched as if she were fighting a smile.

"So—do we have a deal?"

"I don't know. Are you going to be okay with…working for me now?"

"It's still my house," Jillian protested.

"Yes. But we're not talking about design decisions. You're

asking to join my crew, small though it may be now, so that means you work for me."

Jillian was silent for so long that Wil thought she was going to refuse. Then she stuck out her hand and said, "Okay."

"Good." After a brief handshake, Wil had to force herself to release Jillian's hand. But even then the feel of Jillian's slender fingers and soft skin remained.

"So what's first on the agenda?"

"Have you ever used a wet saw?"

"No."

Wil handed her a pair of safety glasses. "Put these on. I'll teach you."

❖

"In here." Wil entered the bathroom and Jillian followed.

The room was still a work in progress, but already Jillian could see the potential. A new pedestal sink had replaced the stock vanity, and later she would hang a wood-framed mirror over it. The claw-foot tub sat under the frosted window, but the plumbing hadn't been hooked up yet.

Jillian stepped into the shower stall and crouched to examine the wall. Tracy had installed the first row of tile yesterday and let it set overnight. That morning Wil had tiled the lower quarter of the stall.

"This is going to look great." She ran her fingers lightly over the tile, pleased with the color. The gentle striations in the gray tone added depth, and the dark slate grout she'd selected would complement it well.

Jillian straightened and found Wil standing beside her. Suddenly they were face-to-face in the small space and Jillian wondered where all the air in the room had gone. Wil's mouth was at eye level and Jillian couldn't help staring at it. She barely smothered a moan as she remembered the feel of those soft lips. Gray dust smudged the side of Wil's neck and when, without thinking, Jillian rubbed her fingers over it, she felt Wil's pulse trip.

"You—ah, you do good work." Forcing her fingers from Wil's skin, she touched the wall instead. Her chest felt tight and her voice sounded breathy.

"I haven't had any complaints." Wil's slow smile said she knew how affected Jillian was.

"I don't suppose you have. And you certainly won't get any from me." Jillian needed to touch her again.

But when she raised her hand, Wil stepped back. Inside the shower, she had no place to go and her back hit the wall.

"We'd better get started on this tile," Wil practically stuttered.

Jillian figured it wouldn't take much to seduce Wil. Hell, they were halfway there just from the heat that flared between them every time their eyes met. But now that their crew was basically nonexistent, and Jillian's planned open-house date was looming closer, letting anything happen between them wasn't a good idea. They needed to work together without any potential of added tension. She shoved aside the quick thought that making love to Wil here against the bathroom wall would surely release some tension. "That's not what I need," she muttered.

"What?"

"Nothing." She clapped her hands together. "Show me what we're doing."

"Okay, hand me that trowel." Wil blinked at the quick change in mood. When Jillian had touched her, it took every ounce of her will not to gather her in her arms and kiss her until they both melted onto the floor. But then the heaviness between them lifted as Jillian seemed to change gears easily.

Deciding she could summon at least as much self-control as Jillian, Wil knelt and picked up a trowel. She showed Jillian how to apply an even layer of thin-set mortar as an adhesive. Then, using spacers to keep the rows even, she pressed the tiles to the wall.

"I can do this," Jillian said.

Wil sat back and watched for a moment, smiling when Jillian bit her lip in concentration as she placed the tile. She'd expected anger, even resistance when she told Jillian about the problem with her crew. And she'd seen them both flash in Jillian's eyes, but what she hadn't foreseen was how quickly Jillian recovered. Logic won out, and Jillian moved smoothly into determination. Her insistence that she work alongside Wil was admirable, and probably practical, if they had any hope of finishing on time. But though she might enjoy the closeness to Jillian, letting a client work on her own project still stung Wil's pride.

❖

"Does your daughter live in a small town?"

"Heavens, no. She couldn't wait to get out of here." Rose settled into a chair in the deep shade of her porch while Jillian, seeking the warmth of the morning sun, rested against the railing nearby.

"City living can be attractive. There are many more conveniences, more options." Jillian appreciated the variety of takeout, movies, and theater within a few blocks of her condo.

"Dear, I'm seventy-one years old. I don't need options. I

have a granddaughter and two beautiful great-grandchildren I rarely see. I have far too many regrets in this life, and I don't want not being a part of their life to be one more."

"I know what you mean. When I was packing up Aunt Mary's things, I realized I'd missed knowing a part of my family, and it made me sad."

Rose smiled wistfully. "Mary was certainly worth knowing."

"What was she like?"

"Stubborn. She was the most pigheaded person I ever met. And far too practical. Good Lord, getting that woman to do anything spontaneous was a chore. But she was also kind, honest, and very generous." Rose smiled at Jillian. "And now that I've met you, I would say those traits run in the family."

"Only the good ones," Jillian quipped.

"They're all good ones."

"That's nice of you to say. Why didn't they have any children?"

"I'd heard they were trying. I guess it just didn't happen."

"You two didn't remain friends?"

"You know how it goes, people grow apart. She was married then. She spent her time with her husband, not out running around with us single gals."

Rose wrung her hands in her lap, and when she lifted her eyes, Jillian thought she saw the shine of unshed tears. But she didn't feel comfortable questioning Rose. Perhaps the loss of her friendship with Mary was one of those regrets she'd spoken of.

After a brief silence, Rose changed the subject. "How are the renovations coming along?"

"Wil had to send the rest of her crew over to the school. So she and I are working on it together."

"I'm surprised she went for that."

Jillian smiled recalling how Wil had clung to her stubbornness even when logic won out. "She required some convincing."

"I imagine she would. Wilhelmina is prideful."

"I get that. She acts as if she has something to prove to the people in this town."

Rose seemed hesitant.

"I don't mean to invade her privacy. She just seems so focused on not being seen as less than others. And in my experience that kind of determination comes from somewhere." Jillian shifted and rested her other hip against the rail, feeling the pull of sore muscles with every movement. Nearly a week of the hardest work Jillian had ever done left her falling exhaustedly into bed every night.

"Her grandfather was not regarded highly in Redmond. He wasn't a nice man, to anyone, including his wife and son. He, and by extension Johnson and Son, had a reputation for shoddy work and making his employees cut corners if it saved a dime."

"That's fairly common among contractors. Though not desirable."

"In a small town that type of reputation is pretty hard to live down. Bud made some strides toward changing it, even through some lean times."

"And Wil has inherited that quest." Jillian was beginning to understand some of what motivated Wil.

Rose nodded. "Inherited it, and made it her life's work. You won't find a more hardworking, honest person in this entire town. And even though everyone already knows it, she seems intent on proving it over and over again."

"She thinks people are constantly judging her," Jillian guessed.

"That's one theory. Feeling inferior can become so deeply ingrained that it's difficult to overcome even when it's not warranted."

Thinking about everything she knew about Wil, Jillian doubted she was actually inferior to anyone. She was trustworthy, valued people over possessions, and genuinely cared about improving her town. In Jillian's experience, there weren't a lot of people like that left these days.

Chapter Ten

Jillian's shoes clicked on the kitchen tile as she walked slowly through the room. The finished project looked like something out of a magazine, far exceeding her original vision. Jillian never spent much time in a kitchen, but she warmed when she thought about Wil moving competently around the space. She'd been watching Wil work for several weeks now, and more than once she'd caught herself studying Wil's hands. Her broad palms and long fingers were surprisingly graceful and strong at the same time. They were confident and efficient, her movements purposeful, and Jillian imagined they would be the same if she was preparing a meal. She didn't need to imagine those same talented hands on her skin. The memory was as vivid as if they'd awakened together that very morning.

Jillian got two bottles of water out of the refrigerator and wandered into the dining room. There was still work to be done here. The crown molding along one wall had been replaced. After making a few repairs, Wil's electrician had signed off on all the wiring.

When she reached the living room she crossed to the fireplace. The mantel was in good condition, but the brick hearth had needed to be restored. Jillian had opted to replace it instead with fieldstone, and Wil had completed that transformation while Jillian finished some painting in other rooms.

Wil walked into the living room at the same time Jillian settled on the couch. "The bathroom is completely done. I just installed the last towel bar."

Wil dropped onto the sofa next to Jillian with a sigh. They'd been putting in long hours every day for two weeks, but it was worth it. Jillian was a quick study and had thrown herself into the work, doing her best to ignore the sexual energy that constantly sizzled between them. Now, even with the loss of three members of Wil's crew, they had finished only a few days behind Wil's original schedule.

"I don't think I've ever worked this hard," Jillian said, handing over one of the water bottles.

Wil leaned back into the cushions and took a long drink, emptying a third of the bottle. "Yeah. Hey, since you're looking for a job, I think Dad's got a crew you could join."

"Funny. I'll leave the manual labor to someone else in the future." Jillian examined her hands. She'd broken three nails this week and she didn't think her skin had ever been this rough.

"Not really a get-your-hands-dirty type, huh?"

"Not at all."

They fell quiet and Jillian closed her eyes. She could easily go to sleep without caring that Wil lounged beside her.

"Let's go out." Wil's voice pulled her out of her trance.

"No thanks. All I want to do is take a shower and get in bed."

"Come on, we're done. We should celebrate."

"Wil, I'm exhausted."

Wil pulled her to her feet and guided her toward the hall

leading to the bedrooms. "Go take that shower and get dressed. I'll meet you back here in an hour and take you to the Ranch and show you what a Saturday night in Redmond is like."

"Okay." She *was* curious about what a night out with Wil would be like.

"See you in an hour," Wil said, just before she closed the front door.

Jillian nodded and headed down the hall. She went to the bedroom closet and pushed hangers aside one by one.

"What does one wear to a redneck bar?" she wondered aloud. Not expecting to do a lot of socializing, she hadn't brought much more than a couple of business suits and clothes to work in. But she finally settled on dark jeans and a boldly colored scoop-neck shirt.

She showered quickly, dressed, and applied light makeup. Deciding to let her hair fall freely over her shoulders, she brushed it until it shone.

"What's wrong with you? It's not a date," she muttered as she checked her reflection in the mirror and smoothed a hand over her hair. The hollow disappointment that followed this reminder was unexpected.

❖

As Wil steered into the parking lot of Rambles Ranch, Jillian commented on the assortment of SUVs, sedans, and minivans among the expected pickup trucks.

A row of chrome-clad motorcycles flanked one side of the door.

"Do you ride?" she asked as Wil parked in one of few remaining spots.

"No," Wil said emphatically.

"Really? Because I can picture you dressed in black leather on a big Harley."

"I don't like motorcycles. Don't get me wrong, they look cool. But I have no desire to ride one." Wil had seen one too many idiots lose control and end up sliding across asphalt. "You look surprised."

"Well, I just—ah—you…"

Understanding the reason for the quick flush rising up Jillian's neck, Wil let her stammer uncomfortably for a second before she interrupted. "Why, Miss Sealy, you weren't stereotyping me. Were you?"

"Not stereotyping, exactly." *Fantasizing is more like it.* She'd been imagining clinging to Wil on the back of a bike. Not once had she ever thought the smell of leather and exhaust could be an aphrodisiac, but if Wil's body filled that leather, she might consider it so. She hoped the lust pumping through her wasn't evident in her voice. To escape Wil's amused expression, Jillian pushed her door open and slid out of the truck. She cleared her throat and said, "Busy place."

"There aren't a lot of places to go on Saturday night. The teenagers hang out at the quarry on the weekends."

"They don't get caught?" Jillian asked as they fell into step together.

Wil shrugged. "Kids have been going down there since I was that age. I guess as long as there's no trouble, the cops leave them alone."

Jillian bumped her shoulder against Wil's. "So, you used to hang out there. Did you have a car?"

"Usually I ended up borrowing Dad's old truck. Of course, I doubt he knew where I was taking it or what I was doing in it."

"What were you doing?"

"You know what kids do—trying to be cool, drinking, playing our music loud."

It was nearly dusk, not quite dark enough to trigger the lights in the parking lot, but a row of lantern-shaped path lights illuminated the shadows of the sidewalk next to the building.

Jillian threaded her arm through Wil's. "Did you have a girlfriend?"

They reached the front door, and as Wil grabbed the handle she paused and answered quietly. "No." She opened the door, and if she said anything else it was lost in the mix of music and voices that spilled out.

"Why not?" Jillian persisted, raising her voice to compete with the noise. "I bet you had a ton of girls chasing you."

"No. I wasn't even sure what it meant to be gay back then, and I definitely didn't have any role models around. It wasn't easy to be out in such a small town. I was just an awkward kid who was scared of being different and wanted my peers to like me."

As they walked inside and were immediately surrounded by people, Jillian didn't pursue the subject.

The decor was over the top, from the split-rail fence flanking the doors to the large milk cans acting as stools at the bar. Jillian was actually disappointed not to find a sawdust floor.

"What are you drinking?" Wil bent close to be heard over the music.

"Beer is fine."

Wil signaled the bartender and Jillian surveyed the diverse crowd. Men in ties with their shirtsleeves rolled up and commuters stopping for a drink after their one-hour drive from the nearest city milled about among men in jeans and work shirts. At the bar, a few women scanned the crowd a little too casually, and Jillian guessed they were sizing up the males. Near the dance floor a group of women filled two tables, clearly there to socialize together as opposed to seeking company.

"Wil," a voice boomed from behind them. Jillian turned to find Bill leaning against the bar. Today he wore a dingy baseball cap and his T-shirt bore the Van Halen logo. "And Miss Jillian, it's good to see you again."

"Hi, Bill."

"Hey, Billy." Wil handed Jillian a bottle of beer and greeted him with a handshake that turned into a half hug.

"We've got a booth over there if you ladies would like to join us." He hooked a thumb over his shoulder.

Wil looked at Jillian. "You mind?"

"Lead the way."

"Fellas, meet Jillian Sealy," Bill called as they approached a large booth full of guys.

Jillian tried to keep up as he called out names and each man raised a hand in greeting, but she was quickly lost. Two men cleared out of one side of the booth and pulled up chairs from other tables. Wil gestured Jillian in, then slid in behind her.

"Make room," Bill said, moments before he squeezed in beside Wil.

"Sorry," Wil mumbled as she was sandwiched between them. She stretched her arm along the back of the seat behind Jillian. "We can sit somewhere else."

"It's okay." Jillian braced her hand on Wil's leg and shifted in an effort to ease the tight fit.

Jillian's fingers were pressing high on Wil's thigh and she froze as their gazes collided. She caught her fingernails on the seam on the inside of Wil's jeans and squeezed her leg. Wil's eyes darkened and she moistened her lower lip. The table hid

Jillian's actions, and she could have easily slipped her hand up to cup Wil. Her hand trembled with the effort of containing the uncharacteristic impulse. Wil covered it with her own and said something under her breath.

"What?"

"Nothing."

Jillian felt the whisper of that word against her cheek and realized if she turned her head only a few inches, she could kiss Wil. She wanted to, badly. And despite the logical reasons why she shouldn't, only the five men crowded around them stopped her.

❖

"Another beer, Wil?" One of the guys reached across the table, grabbed their empties, and passed them to the waiting server.

Wil nodded and turned to Jillian. "Do you want another?"

"I've had three already." Jillian was light-headed. It had been a while since she'd had more than the occasional Manhattan with dinner.

"So, that's a no?"

"Okay. One more, but that's my limit."

Wil held up two fingers and the server headed for the bar. "Are you okay? You're not bored, are you?" Wil asked, bending close.

"I'm fine. Your friends are…interesting." Jillian glanced at the men carrying on around them. They seemed like nice-enough guys, though a few were a little rough around the edges for Jillian's taste. And the Ranch lacked the sophistication of Jillian's usual watering hole in Cincinnati. But feeling Wil's body pressed firmly against the length of her side was enough to distract her. Wil's thigh was warm against hers even through two layers of denim, and Wil's arm still rested along the back of her neck.

"Well, other than Bill, they're not exactly friends, more like—"

"Drinking buddies."

"For lack of a better term, yes. We spend so much time working, it's nice to be able to unwind every once in a while."

"What else do you do to…unwind?" Jillian hadn't meant the question to sound so much like a come-on.

Wil's smile brought butterflies to Jillian's stomach. "Well, I don't know. What did *you* have in mind?"

"I—uh—meant—"

"I know what you meant, but I couldn't resist. Summers are our busiest time, so I don't have a ton of free time. But I do a little woodworking or go down to the lake."

A sudden burst of laughter drew their attention back to the other occupants of their table.

"What about it, Wil, you wanna ride tonight?" Bill asked, loud enough for everyone to hear.

Wil shook her head. "I haven't done that since I was too young to know better."

"Done what?" Jillian asked, feeling left out.

"That." Wil pointed toward the back of the bar where Jillian saw a group gathered around a roped-off circle. In the center, a mechanical bull gyrated and dipped, trying to unseat the lanky man clinging to its back.

"Come on, Wil. I'll put twenty bucks on the bull." One of the men slapped a meaty hand with a crisp bill trapped under it on the table in front of them.

"I'm in," Bill said, throwing his money down. "But I know better than to bet against Wil. My money's on her."

Several other bills landed on the table as men shouted out their bets.

Jillian laughed. "You've actually done that?"

"What's so funny?" Wil seemed offended.

"Nothing. I just can't picture it."

"Well, let me help you out with that." She downed the rest of her beer, shoved Bill out of the way, and strode toward the back of the bar followed by an entourage of men egging her on.

"Wil." Jillian hurried to catch up and grasped her arm, but Wil pulled it away. "Wil, what are you doing?"

Wil reached the edge of the ring and nodded at the man operating the controls. He grinned and lifted his chin in return.

"I didn't mean—" Jillian flinched as the current rider was flung off and landed several feet away. Despite the foam pads lining the floor, he was slow to get up. "You're not really going to get on that thing, are you?"

Their eyes met and stubborn pride burned in Wil's. She unbuttoned her shirt and slipped it from her shoulders, revealing a gray tank top that hugged her small, firm breasts and flat stomach. "Hold this."

Jillian took the shirt and watched, stunned, as Wil walked over to talk to the operator. Then she climbed up on the worn leather and grasped the handle, the muscles of her forearm bunching as she set her grip. She squared her strong shoulders, then raised her left hand over her head and nodded.

The bull began to rock, slowly at first. Wil alternately folded herself over the front of the machine and stretched back, reaching her arm up and back. Her denim-encased thighs hardened with the effort of keeping her body centered, and her upper body flowed with the rhythm of the bucking bull. The operator jerked the machine hard to the right. Wil's chin was tucked to her chest and her face was a study in concentration as she seemed to anticipate the spin and managed to stay astride.

Jillian would never have thought she would find anything remotely arousing about a woman riding a mechanical bull, but as she stood at the edge of the ring, her entire body buzzed. Though Wil's attention never wavered from the bull, Jillian could feel a thread of energy connecting them. Wil had reacted instantly to Jillian's amusement earlier and now she was showing off. For her. Obvious displays of bravado normally didn't do it for her. But seeing Wil's raw power meld sinuously with grace, combined with the knowledge that it was meant to impress her, turned her on. Molten heat flowed along her limbs and pooled between her thighs.

The bull made another sharp spin and Wil's hips slid against the impossible centrifugal force. Jillian braced herself, expecting to see Wil flung off, but somehow she held on. Her arm strained against her own weight, and Jillian was hit with the memory of those same muscles flexing beneath her grasping hand as Wil stroked her. Jillian watched Wil's hips and, suddenly, she wanted to feel that hard body rocking against hers again.

The operator seemed to take no mercy on Wil, grinning as he frantically worked the controls. But before he could unseat her, a horn sounded and he held his hands up. The bull slowed and, without power driving the hydraulics, sank lower. Raising both arms, Wil slid her leg over the machine and dropped to the ground. Amid whistles and shouts, she slapped the back of the bull.

As Wil approached, she responded to the high fives and pats on the back, but her gaze was locked on Jillian. Caught off guard by her own reaction, Jillian sought retreat behind familiar aloof indifference, but was unable to summon it. She was entranced by Wil's eyes, by the glassy high of triumph in them, and even more by the way they seemed to seek her approval.

"Did you accomplish what you'd hoped to?" Jillian asked, tossing Wil's shirt at her.

Wil caught it smoothly and slipped it on, but left it unbuttoned. "You tell me. Were you impressed?"

"Was that your goal?"

"Yes."

The simple honesty seemed at odds with her cocky strut and the macho display just moments ago. Wil steered Jillian to the side as the next challenger, cheered on the by the crowd, climbed on the bull.

"You could have been hurt." Jillian took Wil's hand and examined her callused palm. She caressed her fingers over Wil's wrist and powerful forearm.

"I'm tougher than that. It takes a lot more than some old mechanical bull to break me."

A roar from the crowd accompanied the new rider's quick fall.

When Jillian traced the scar along the outside of Wil's arm and met her eyes, Wil said, "Freshly cut thin-gauge sheet metal. That stuff is razor sharp."

Jillian touched one of the larger nicks on the back of her hand, next to her thumb.

"Nail gun. That one could've been a lot worse."

She turned Wil's hand over and lightly scratched her fingernail over a knot nestled in the fleshy area just below her ring finger.

"Monster splinter." Wil grinned. "I lost a lot of blood that day."

Realizing Wil was teasing her, Jillian dropped her hand.

"I've got some other scars, and with a bit more privacy I'd be happy to show you." The words slipped out before Wil could stop them. Jillian's touch short-circuited the connection between her brain and her mouth. The swift darkening of Jillian's eyes reminded Wil that Jillian had already seen every inch of her body.

"Really?" Jillian slipped two fingers down the side of Wil's neck, rested them in the hollow between her collarbones, then angled close until her lips were within inches of Wil's ear. "If I say yes, do you plan to make good on that promise?"

"I'd love to." The bull ride still had adrenaline singing through Wil's veins, and Jillian's sexy tone and hot breath in her ear amped her up even further.

Just then she didn't care if Jillian thought she was beneath her or that Jillian was in Redmond temporarily. The feel of Jillian's fingers wandering down the center of her chest and her own heart thudding beneath them nearly silenced any practical objection she could offer. Images of taking Jillian home and making love to her flooded Wil's head, but she was still lucid enough to know that was the worst idea she'd had all night.

"Jillian," Wil said as Jillian slipped a hand down her stomach.

"Yes?" Jillian curled her fingers around Wil's belt buckle and tugged her closer. Jillian's breasts brushed hers, and when her nipples tightened in response, she pulled her shirt closed and buttoned it.

"Do you want to go someplace else?"

"Yes."

CHAPTER ELEVEN

"This isn't exactly what I thought you meant by *someplace else*." Jillian turned on the seat of Wil's truck to look at her. Despite the darkened interior, the flickering images on the screen in front of them cast a harsh light across Wil's features.

"I promised you'd experience a typical Redmond weekend. You can't do that without catching the late show at the drive-in." Wil turned on the radio and tuned it to the proper frequency to hear the movie's audio. "You don't have to hang a speaker on the window anymore, but it still has a nostalgic feel, doesn't it?"

Jillian shrugged. "I've never actually been to a drive-in."

"Really? When I was a kid, I used to come here with my mom and dad."

Wil hadn't thought about the days before her parents' divorce in years. For so long it seemed like her only memories were of the fighting, her mother leaving, then Wil and her father working nonstop to get ahead. But now she remembered there had actually been happy times when she was younger. Occasionally, on summer nights, they would pile into the old Impala and come to this very spot. Of course back then it was little more than a field with a big screen in the middle. They'd added another screen and a concession stand in the intervening years.

Her mother made popcorn and packed cold drinks in a small cooler. And when it got chilly they huddled under a blanket. Wil could still feel the scratch of the wool against her neck and smell her mother's heavy floral perfume.

"My parents worked a lot when we were young," Jillian said.

"What do they do?"

"They're both doctors."

"Impressive. You didn't want to follow in their footsteps?"

"Medicine never interested me. Plus, I'm squeamish about blood and needles. My brother is a surgeon, and one of us was enough for them."

"What do they think about your chosen career?"

"Well, it wasn't quite upper-middle-class enough for them until I really started earning the big commissions. My father would prefer that I handle strictly lucrative commercial accounts."

"And you don't want to?"

Jillian considered her answer, thinking that for the first time she understood why she liked residential real estate. "Don't get me wrong, I enjoy the income associated with commercial deals. But there's something satisfying about helping someone find a home where so many of their memories will be built."

"I knew it. You're really a romantic at heart."

Jillian had never thought of herself as such. She was too practical to be romantic. She'd accepted that she likely would never have the blazing passion that women swooned over. "No. I'll admit to being a tad sentimental, though."

"So you don't want to be swept off your feet by a conquering hero," Wil said.

Jillian shrugged. "There's no point in thinking about it. That stuff only happens in books."

"Maybe you're right. But there are other kinds of romance."

"Like what?"

"Small gestures. As obvious as bringing you flowers when I know you've had a bad day. Or as understated as a simple concession to something you want even if it's not my preference, because it would make you happy."

"Giving in. That's romance?"

"It can be."

Jillian jerked her head around at the sound of a scream. "Did I mention I don't like scary movies?"

"This movie isn't that scary." Truthfully, Wil hadn't paid attention to what was showing. When they'd left the bar, she'd wanted to spend more time with Jillian, but she was afraid to be alone with her. She'd driven here hoping that if she stuck to a public place she wouldn't forget why she shouldn't sleep with Jillian again. But shrouded in the darkened interior of the truck, she realized she hadn't thought her choice of entertainment through quite enough. It certainly felt as if they were alone, and the urge to hold Jillian was strong.

"By definition, if it has a man who kills people by bludgeoning them with a shovel, it's a scary movie," Jillian argued.

"But it's so predictable. Besides, it's not even realistic." Another shriek pierced the air, and Jillian jumped. Wil turned down the volume and held out her arm. "Come over here."

Without hesitation, Jillian slid to the middle of the seat, lifting one leg over the gearshift. Wil draped her arm around

Jillian's shoulders and tried not to react when she buried her face against her neck while the man with the shovel claimed another victim.

"Is it over yet?"

Wil glanced at the screen just as a spurt of fake blood covered the killer's overalls. She waited until the scene cut away to a less gory setting. "Yeah, it's over."

Jillian glanced tentatively at the screen, then turned an accusing glare on Wil.

Wil raised her hands in innocence. "I didn't know what kind of movie it was. *And* how would I even know you didn't like them?"

"Okay. I'll give you a pass for now. But you can't use that excuse next time."

"Deal." Wil forced a smile, wondering why it should bother her that there probably wouldn't be a next time.

❖

"Come sit with me for a while." Jillian circled the truck, took Wil's hand, and tugged her toward the house.

They sat on the third step, their shoulders touching. Wil drew her knees up and rested her forearms on them. Jillian tilted her head and Wil visually traced the line of her neck until it disappeared in the neckline of her shirt.

"Have you ever seen so many stars?" Jillian looked at Wil and caught her staring.

"Well, yeah, I have."

"Oh, that's right. This is a normal view for you."

"It's the same sky. Do you have too many buildings in your way to see it?"

"Maybe. Or maybe I just don't take the time to appreciate it. But the air is clearer and the stars seem brighter here."

Jillian propped her elbows on the step behind her, and Wil did the same. The stars spilled across the black velvet background like a scattering of brilliant diamonds. In that moment, Jillian couldn't think of anything more important than stretching out to catch a handful of that glitter. The priorities she'd been struggling with since arriving in Tennessee slipped away, and nothing she had in Ohio was as important as sitting on these stairs with Wil.

"I guess I take it for granted," Wil murmured. "I can't remember the last time I even looked at them."

"Well, you should stop and—"

"Please don't say smell the roses."

"I was going to say see the beauty."

"That's just as bad."

When Wil looked at her again, Jillian purposefully let her gaze caress her face. Wil's eyes were luminous. The silvery moonlight washed out her normally tan skin, and if she didn't have such strong features she would have had an almost ethereal quality. As it was, the contrast of her thick, dark lashes and brows brought to mind a dramatic charcoal rendering. Jillian was so entranced, she spoke without thinking. "There's plenty of beauty to be found without staring up in the air."

"That's certainly a smooth line." Wil's voice sounded shaky.

Jillian angled her body toward Wil's. "It isn't a line," she said softly. "You're stunning." Unable to resist the urge to touch her, Jillian edged closer. When Wil began to slide away, Jillian grabbed her lapels. "It's just a kiss, Wil."

"No. It's not *just* a kiss."

Jillian wasn't detoured. She wasn't thinking about anything other than the heat building within her. She moved closer and framed Wil's face in her hands.

"Jillian, please." Wil grasped her forearms.

Jillian slid her fingers deep into Wil's hair. "Please what?" She pressed her lips to Wil's jaw.

Wil's hands tightened on Jillian's arms. "Please don't." Her voice was a strangled moan.

Jillian paused. "Don't? Are you saying you don't want me to kiss you right now?" she whispered.

"I can't stop wanting you."

Jillian met her eyes and found them soft and vulnerable. "You say that like it's a bad thing."

"I don't want to want you. This would have been so much easier if I didn't." The stab of desire in Wil's chest made her more forthcoming than usual. She clung to Jillian's arms, but though she could easily have pulled Jillian's hands away, she didn't.

"This?"

"Working with you. Seeing you every day." They had chemistry, Wil would admit that. But there was more, which she was hesitant to put a voice to. The tenderness she'd felt when Jillian was sick, the respect for the way Jillian stepped in when she lost her crew, and the warmth expanding in her chest scared her more than any physical attraction. Jillian would be leaving soon, and she needed to remember that fact.

Jillian's fingers stilled against her skin, and Wil had only a moment to absorb their warmth before they were withdrawn.

"Is that why you keep running from me?" Jillian asked quietly.

"I do not."

"Yes. You do. Oh, you aren't now because you don't have your crew to hide behind. It's okay that we had sex, but when we connect on a more emotional level, you trot out that I'm-not-as-good-as-you bullshit." Jillian was beginning to see that quite the opposite might be true.

"I don't want to talk about this." Wil retreated verbally, further proving Jillian's accusation.

"I know. But I want to."

"Jillian, drop it."

"Why?" She reached up to touch Wil's face again, but Wil grasped her wrist and held it away from her.

"Because I don't want us to connect."

"Why not?" Jillian's heart pounded and she wondered if Wil could feel it in the pulse under her fingers.

"I know what you think of me, Jillian. And I'm not interested in being your charity case." Wil shoved Jillian's hand away.

"You can't seriously believe I think that."

Wil shrugged. "I'm a handyman's daughter. I grew up in this town basically on welfare. I've been dealing with that attitude my whole life." Jillian hated the resignation in her eyes.

"I should have apologized to you that day. I don't see you that way. I'm a private person, Wil. We'd just had an amazing night, and when I thought Rose could see right through me, I panicked. Are you going to let one misunderstanding keep you from—"

"From what? What exactly are you looking for? Are you planning to settle down here?"

"Is that what you want?" She searched her memory for any indication that Wil might have given that what was between them was more than sexual attraction. Where had she gotten the idea that was all it was? She'd cast Wil as the shallow playgirl, but Wil had never done anything to deserve that assumption. In reality, Jillian was the one who had been so concerned with appearances that she'd insulted Wil rather than face…whatever was between them. Jillian was stunned to think Wil might want something more permanent. And what if she did? Jillian couldn't imagine either of them being happy in the other's world.

"It doesn't matter. I know you're leaving. And I still have my own reasons for not wanting to get involved with you. But none of that changes the fact that I only have to look at you or think about you and I want you."

"Then why shouldn't we enjoy each other?" The proposal was too little too late, and she knew it. But hearing that Wil wanted her so, and the rasp of longing in her voice, made Jillian want to reach out. But she couldn't reach far enough.

"No." Defeat saturated Wil's tone.

Jillian stood. "Okay. Thanks for tonight."

A spring creaked as Jillian opened the screen door, and she stepped inside and let it bang shut behind her. She stood in the darkness and listened until a minute later she heard Wil's truck start. Reminding herself that Wil had her reasons for turning her away didn't alleviate the sting of rejection. She'd offered Wil what she could and had been turned down.

❖

"I finished it a couple nights ago." Wil pressed the remote to open her overhead garage door, then led her father inside.

"Wow. Wil, it's great." Bud crossed to the desk standing in the middle of the space and touched it lightly. "I had no idea you were making it so detailed."

She hadn't initially planned to, but as she worked she'd experimented with small touches of molding and decorative carving, testing her skill. She'd added ornate brass hardware and stained it the color of honey.

"It'll look nice in your office." Her father had been working behind the same banged-up metal desk for as long as she could remember. At first he couldn't afford more, then she supposed it became habit. He'd spent most of his life fixing up other people's houses, but when it came to his own home and office he was content to leave things how they were. His house was still decorated the same as it had been the day his wife had walked out on him.

He nodded and continued to run a hand across the satiny surface.

"Hey, Dad, did Mom ever like it here?" Wil asked cautiously. They rarely talked about her mother. When she was younger, he didn't want to, and now she was just accustomed to not mentioning when she'd spoken to her.

"She said she did, at first."

Her mother had been living in D.C. when they'd met while her father was on vacation. He'd courted her long-distance and within six months had convinced her to move to Redmond.

"So what happened?"

He shrugged. "I guess some are just country folks, and some aren't."

"And you don't think they can change?" Wil had seen refusal slide across Jillian's features the night before when she'd asked if she planned to settle down in Redmond. Like Wil's mother, she would wither in a small town.

"Why don't you ask your mother these questions?" Some of the old bitterness seeped into his words.

"'Cause I'm asking you." She and her mother weren't close, and often Wil related to her only out of a sense of obligation. She sensed her mother made an effort to reach out, but Wil would never understand how a mother could leave her child.

"Yeah, well," he circled the desk and grabbed one side, "can you talk and lift at the same time?"

Wil picked up the other end and they carefully carried

it out to the driveway where his old truck was parked. The logo on the side was faded and patches of rust showed through dulled green paint.

"About time for a new truck, isn't it?" Wil rested her side of the desk on the open tailgate, climbed into the bed, and pulled the desk the rest of the way in.

"This one runs just fine."

"The owner of a successful construction company shouldn't be driving this old clunker." Wil jumped to the ground. "All the foremen have nicer trucks than you do. Buy a new one. Call it a tax deduction for next year."

"I suppose I could make this a shop truck. That one we've been using has seen better days." They'd added three new storage buildings in the past five years and often used an old pickup to shuttle supplies between them.

Side by side they leaned against the edge of the still-open tailgate.

"If you'd known how it would end, would you still have asked her to marry you?" Wil steered the conversation back to her mother.

He folded his arms over his chest, clearly uncomfortable with the direction of their conversation. "Yes, I would do it again."

"She broke your heart." Wil remembered how devastated he'd been after her mother left. And sometimes she wondered if that was the reason he hadn't dated since.

He shifted his weight and wrung his hands. "No one goes into a marriage thinking it's going to fail."

"But if she had stayed—"

"We both knew it was over well before that. Nothing's ever so black and white. We had more problems than just geography." He paced across the driveway, rubbing a hand over his scalp.

Feeling abandoned, Wil had made her mother into the bad guy. She'd spent years blaming her mother's inability to adjust to small-town living for the demise of their family. She'd called her mother uncaring and inflexible. But her father had let her. Lost in his own heartache, he hadn't been able to deal with her anger, so eventually she'd just buried her pain beneath so many layers that no one could touch it. And even now, she held her mother at arm's length, as if she could punish her by shutting her out of her life.

"What made you think about all this now?"

"It's nothing, Dad."

"Is something going on with your mother?"

"No." It wasn't about her parents at all.

"Okay." He seemed relieved to be off the hook, but his subject change didn't ease Wil's mind. "How are things at Miss Sealy's? Has she forgiven me for pulling your crew?"

"Yeah, I think she's over it." Wil neglected to mention that she'd had to let Jillian work with her.

"She seems easy to get along with."

Wil laughed. "Easy? Yeah. As long as she gets her way."

"I was out at the school Friday and your girls spoke well of her."

"Of course." Wil agreed without thinking. Despite having criticized her, after they found out Wil had slept with her, the girls seemed to have warmed up to Jillian again. "I've seen the way Tracy looks at her. And supposedly *she's* straight. And don't get me started on Andy and Patti. Jesus, my entire crew was half in love with her."

"Really? Your *entire* crew?"

Her words echoed in her head. Had she just admitted she was in love with Jillian? No. No, she'd said *half* in love. And she'd only been trying to make a point about the girls. She hadn't meant that she was actually…had she?

"Uh, no. It was a figure of speech. I just meant the girls really took to her." She backpedaled quickly and he seemed to buy it.

Distracted by her line of thought, Wil barely responded as he thanked her again for the desk. His truck sputtered to life and she pulled herself together long enough to wave good-bye before crossing to her porch and sinking down on the steps.

She was an idiot. How did this happen? She'd been guarding herself against this very thing since the moment they'd met. *Right. So that's why you slept with her after knowing her for two days. Way to keep your distance.* Distance. That's what she needed now. Wasn't it?

She shoved a hand through her hair. It would be smart to keep any future interactions professional. No more taking Jillian to the Ranch or sitting under the stars with her.

But even as she made this promise, she knew it wouldn't do any good. Staying away from Jillian didn't keep her from thinking about her, wondering what she was doing. It was too late to avoid getting hurt, she was certain of that. Jillian's open house was next weekend. After that she'd be leaving and Wil would deal with missing her then.

Maybe the answer was to spend more time with her. Yes. They were so different that a relationship between them likely wouldn't work out anyway. So she just needed to let the attraction run its course, as quickly as possible. By the time Jillian left, Wil would probably discover some annoying fault and be happy to be rid of her. It was either the most brilliant or the most insane idea she'd ever had.

CHAPTER TWELVE

Two hours later as Wil knocked on Jillian's door, she was still trying to decide which it was. When Jillian opened the door, Wil leaned toward insanity. Jillian had on the same cutoffs she'd worn to paint the kitchen, and this time a pale yellow tank top hugged the swell of her breasts, the arc of her ribs, and the flat plane of her belly. Jillian's exposed arms were firm, Wil guessed from a routine gym regimen, and her creamy skin lacked the uneven tan Wil always seemed to have from working in the sun.

Wil traced her eyes over the flare of Jillian's hips but wrenched them away when she reached her thighs. She had a visceral memory of those very muscles hardening under her hands as Jillian sat in her lap. Wil tried to swallow, despite the fact that all the moisture in her body had flooded to parts south.

Jillian stood completely still while Wil's gaze swept over her and a flush of heat followed in its wake. The path seared back up her body, and as they stared at each other, Jillian didn't even try to hide the images flying through her head. For a moment she allowed herself to wonder if she would rather Wil undress her slowly or tear her clothes off.

Wil was the first to look away, but the current continued to jump between them, snapping like the severed end of a live wire dancing in the air.

"We're going on a picnic," Wil blurted, as if she needed to fill the silence. And Jillian noticed for the first time that her right arm was wrapped around a paper grocery bag and a small cooler dangled from her other hand.

"We are?"

"Yes. It's part of your typical Redmond weekend." Wil shifted the bag and adjusted her grip on the cooler.

"Oh, I'm sorry." Jillian stepped aside. "Come in. Let me take that." She lifted the bag from Wil's arm and led her to the kitchen. "God, this smells great."

"I made fried chicken, potato salad, and biscuits."

"I could get used to you showing up at my door with food." After setting the bag on the counter, she turned and almost ran into Wil.

"Sorry." Wil grasped her upper arms. "For such a roomy house, I seem to get in your way an awful lot."

"Yes. You do." Jillian cleared her throat and took a step back. "I—just give me a minute to change and I'll be ready to go."

Wil gave her a slow perusal. "What's wrong with what you have on?"

"Oh, *now* you don't have a problem with what I'm wearing?"

Wil grinned. "Well, it *is* going to be just you and me. So whatever you're comfortable in is fine."

"Yeah. I think I'll change just the same." Jillian waved a hand toward the bedroom.

Arousal hung in the air between them, seeping into their clothing like the scent of campfire smoke, and lingered to remind Jillian of the moments when the flames had consumed them.

❖

"Where are we?" Jillian asked as Wil steered her truck into a tree-lined gravel drive. She stopped in front of a small house, further dwarfed by the towering trees and vast stretches of green grass that surrounded it.

"My place. It's not much, but it's home."

Jillian slid out of the truck and looked around. Thick woods edged the lawn on three sides, and she imagined in the fall a colorful cocoon would surround the house. If any neighbors were within range, she couldn't see them from here.

"How far does your property go?"

Wil lifted the cooler from the bed of the truck. "About two hundred yards into the trees on either side. The back runs to a clearing near the lake. I thought we could picnic down there."

Jillian searched the tree line for a break that would indicate a road. "How do we get there?"

"On those." Wil pointed at two ATVs sitting side by side near the corner of the carport. One had camouflage paint and black luggage racks on the front and back. The other, a smaller, sportier model, was bright yellow.

"Are you kidding?" Jillian eyed the two machines, wondering if she was about to embarrass herself.

"I told you I like to go down to the lake."

"I thought you meant a peaceful walk on the shore."

Wil grinned. "I guess we have different definitions of peaceful. Have you ever been on one of these?"

"No."

"This one's yours." Wil crossed to the larger one and

stowed their dinner in a cargo box secured to the rack behind the seat.

"I don't want the bigger one."

"It's wider and more stable than mine, and it has an automatic transmission. I've made a few modifications to the other one to kick up the horsepower, so trust me, you don't want that one." Wil smiled and handed her a helmet. "Get on."

Jillian put her left foot on the step on the side nearest her and swung her other leg over the seat.

"The only shifting you have to do is forward or reverse." Wil leaned over and indicated a small shifter in front of Jillian's right knee. Jillian paid close attention as she went through the rest of the controls, showing her the brakes and throttle. When Wil straightened, her arm brushed Jillian's breast, but she apparently didn't notice because when Jillian shivered, she said, "Don't worry, we'll be on flat terrain. It's an easy ride."

She climbed on her ATV and started it. "Follow me," she shouted before she put on her helmet.

Wil rolled forward, obviously going slow to give Jillian a chance to get used to the ATV. Jillian accelerated too quickly, and when her machine jumped forward she released the lever and tried again. This time her progress was smoother and she followed Wil across the backyard toward the trees. As they neared the edge, Jillian could make out a small break in the form of two tire tracks.

Wil glanced back for only a second before plunging into the woods. Jillian followed a bit more cautiously. She knew there was probably plenty of clearance on both sides as she carefully negotiated over roots, stones, and hard-packed dirt, but she felt as if she could reach out and touch the branches flanking the path. Shafts of sunlight pierced the thick canopy overhead, lighting patches of bright green foliage as they stretched toward the ground. The scent of damp earth permeated the air, and moss crept up the sides of tree trunks.

As they emerged from the trees on the other side, a large clearing led to the edge of the lake. Feeling more confident, Jillian punched the accelerator and pulled alongside Wil. When Wil looked over, Jillian smiled inside the full-face helmet and pointed at the shore as if to say, "First one there wins." Wil nodded and Jillian took off with her fast on her heels. She gave it a little more gas and pulled away, enjoying a bit of speed as the wind rushed past.

Halfway across the grassy expanse, she had a considerable lead and was already savoring her win when Wil's engine revved. Before Jillian even had time to glance back, Wil flew by and she realized Wil had just been playing with her.

Wil was already dismounting by the time Jillian pulled alongside her. They'd parked a few feet from the shoreline, where the grass gave way to a sand and rock beach. A slight breeze swept off the lake, carrying with it a musky scent.

"I never had a chance, did I?" Laughing, Jillian dismounted and set her helmet on the seat.

Wil grinned. "My machine was built for speed." She wrapped an arm around Jillian's waist and pulled her closer. "What do I win?"

Thrown off balance, Jillian braced a hand against Wil's chest as her body came into solid contact with Wil's.

"What do you want?" Jillian whispered. When she moistened her lower lip nervously, Wil's heart beat harder under her hand.

"Just a kiss."

"I thought you said it wasn't just a kiss." Testing, Jillian slid her hand up to toy with the ridge of Wil's collarbone. Wil's eyes darkened and her hand caressed the skin beneath the hem of Jillian's shirt.

"Maybe I've decided that it can be."

A tiny thrill traveled Jillian's spine with Wil's words. She tilted her head to accept the inevitable kiss, but Wil released her and turned back to the cargo box on the ATV. She got out the grocery bag, cooler, and a checkered blanket.

"Will you help me with this?" Wil shook out the blanket and Jillian grabbed the opposite side. They spread it in the grass a few feet from the waterline. "Have a seat."

When they were settled side by side Jillian waited for Wil to unpack the food. But instead she stretched her legs out in front of her and propped herself on her elbow.

"Are you enjoying your weekend?" Wil's words were casual, but the heat from a moment ago hadn't faded from her eyes. And her restraint was obvious in the deliberate way she tightened and relaxed her fists, then crossed her ankles.

Jillian mirrored her pose. "Very much."

"I know it's not big-city culture, but—"

"You must really think I'm high maintenance." Jillian edged closer and Wil's gaze flickered down her body. "Do I strike you as hard to please?"

Wil smiled at the innuendo in Jillian's words. "Not in the least." Though she'd changed to khaki shorts, Jillian still wore the yellow tank top. It gapped slightly at her chest, giving Wil a glimpse of cleavage, and she purposely let her eyes linger there. "In fact," Wil traced the back of Jillian's hand where it lay on the blanket between them, "I find you quite easy to please."

"Hmm. And where do you think calling me easy is going to get you?"

"Oh, there's nothing easy about you," Wil murmured as she danced her fingers up Jillian's forearm. Jillian's brow wrinkled, but before she could take offense, Wil went on. "Maybe pleasing you just comes naturally to me."

"You might be right about that." Jillian's voice dropped seductively but also carried a touch of hesitation, as if she was trying to figure out where Wil was going with the flirtation.

Wil couldn't blame her, since she didn't know herself. She only knew that she liked teasing Jillian, liked touching her. And though her earlier discovery while talking to her father should have freaked her out, it didn't. Knowing she would hurt when Jillian left and having given herself permission to spend time with her anyway freed her.

"And what would please you now?" Wil touched Jillian's neck, then let her fingers dip into the cleavage to stroke her soft skin.

Jillian captured her hand and guided it to her breast. "Don't you know?"

"I've got a few ideas." Wil eased Jillian back to lie on the soft flannel of the blanket. Her hand still cradled Jillian's breast, and Jillian's nipple pressed eagerly into her palm.

Without hesitation, Wil leaned over and claimed her mouth, aggressively at first. And Jillian responded just as fervently, sucking Wil's tongue as she thrust it inside. Then Wil gentled the kiss, easing back to softly caress her lips.

"Please, don't stop," Jillian whispered, clutching Wil's shoulders.

She wouldn't stop. Couldn't have if she'd tried. For weeks she'd been fighting this attraction, beating back awareness at every turn, but she no longer needed to. Whatever happened after this day, she would have this moment. She would have Jillian on a blanket in the sun.

She pushed up Jillian's tank top and touched her warm, flat stomach, spreading her hand to span nearly the width of her torso. Her broad, work-roughened hand made Jillian's skin look even more pale and feminine. "Like porcelain," Wil murmured.

Jillian framed her face and pulled her closer. She bit Wil's lower lip then kissed her chin. "Except I don't break easily."

She sat up and lifted Wil's shirt over her head, then tossed it aside. As she reached for the hem of her own shirt, Wil's hands were there dragging it upward and off. Wil's eyes roamed over her body, alight with hunger. Wil bent and drew one of Jillian's nipples into her mouth, while she cupped her other breast and pinched the nipple lightly. Jillian arched, pushing firmly into Wil's touch.

The gentle suction and the ministrations of Wil's fingers tugged a string connecting Jillian's nipples to several inches of sensitive flesh between her legs. Her clit swelled and pulsed heavily. Pulling away for only a moment, she shed the rest of her clothing, then scooted closer and draped her legs over Wil's and around her hips so they sat face-to-face.

Wil trailed her fingers over Jillian's body, deliberately tracing her curves. Seeming to have infinite patience, Wil circled maddeningly low on Jillian's stomach before veering away. Jillian needed more, harder. She needed to be possessed as Wil had done so many weeks before, filling her and making her feel as if she'd finally found a missing piece of herself.

"I won't break," she repeated, and took Wil's hand and pressed it to her center. When Wil didn't move, she slipped a finger between Wil's to rub over her aching clit.

Wil's knowing smile said she was fully aware of what Jillian was trying to do. She pulled her hand away, taking Jillian's with it, and said, "It's my turn to lead."

"I need you to touch me." Jillian tried to guide Wil's hand back.

"When I say." Wil kissed her neck. "Where I say." She wrapped her arms around Jillian and caressed her back.

As Jillian's hips shifted restlessly between her thighs, Wil continued her slow exploration. She would not be hurried. Jillian's struggle with her self-control flashed across her face. Her eyes were dark with arousal and she pulled her lower lip between her teeth.

"You just wait until it's my turn," she growled in warning as Wil feathered her fingers down her stomach to the place where the patch of curls began.

"I can't wait." Grinning, Wil grasped Jillian's hips and pulled them closer.

"It seems that you can." Jillian's words ended on a moan as Wil trailed her fingers through the wetness, grazing her clit. "Wil."

The roughly spoken word carried a plea Wil could satisfy. This time as she stroked along the folds, she applied more pressure, lingering when Jillian's thighs quivered. And when she curled two fingers inside, Jillian sighed and tilted her hips, giving Wil better access. Jillian immediately tried to increase the pace but Wil controlled her from the inside, stroking long and slow, then pulling out until her fingertips teased Jillian's opening. And just when Jillian's hands fisted in frustration, Wil sank back in.

She kept this pace, even when her own throbbing body demanded attention. Her focus remained on Jillian's pleasure, on her gasping cries for more, and the undulation of Jillian's hips against her hand.

"Please, Wil." Jillian leaned back, arching until her shoulder blades rested against Wil's legs. With measured strokes, Wil drew Jillian to the edge and only then did she press her thumb over the ridge of swollen tissue surrounding Jillian's clitoris. Jillian whispered, "Oh, yes, there."

As Jillian's body tensed and drew her deeper with every stroke, Wil bent to press her mouth to the center of Jillian's chest, just below her breasts. One of Jillian's hands tangled in her hair and the other grasped the back of her neck. When Jillian cried out and shuddered, she clutched Wil tightly to her.

As her body relaxed Wil continued to hold her, bowed over her and immersed in the salty taste of her skin and the scent of her arousal. Though she didn't utter a sound, she mouthed the words "I love you" against Jillian's skin.

After a moment she straightened, took Jillian's hands, and pulled her up too. Not ready to lose the connection, Wil circled her arms around Jillian's waist and held her close. She kissed Jillian's neck, feeling the tickle of her fragrant hair against her face.

Jillian played her fingers in Wil's hair, sweeping stubborn strands off her forehead. She traced the shell of Wil's ear and Wil shivered.

"Why are you still wearing your jeans?" Jillian teased against Wil's neck.

"Because you didn't take them off me." Wil kissed Jillian's bare shoulder.

"Well, that can be rectified."

Wil smiled. "Are you hungry?" she murmured. When she drew back to meet Jillian's eyes she was pleased with the haze of fulfillment that clouded them.

"Starving." Jillian's gaze was fixed on Wil's mouth and she clearly wasn't thinking about food. "But I'd rather take care of you first."

Wil debated the few minutes she knew it would take for Jillian to bring her to orgasm. She'd been almost there as Jillian had climaxed. But she decided she'd rather let her need simmer until they'd eaten. The steady throb of arousal felt good, and she wanted to spend their meal imagining the many ways Jillian might ease it. "I'm okay for now."

"Sure?" Jillian asked lazily.

"Mmm-hmm. Sorry. I let the chicken get cold."

Jillian laughed. "I don't think an apology is necessary." She touched a finger to Wil's chin. "Luckily, fried chicken is just as good cold."

CHAPTER THIRTEEN

Wil drove through the nearly deserted streets of town toward Jillian's house. Her body hummed with satisfaction and her skin felt tight from too much sun. Jillian rode beside her, their linked hands stretched across the expanse of seat between them.

"Where is everyone?" Jillian asked. "It's not that late."

Wil glanced at the clock in the center of the dash. "It's almost nine on Sunday night. Folks are getting ready for work tomorrow, I guess."

For Wil, the day had passed too quickly. After they'd eaten lunch, they had taken a walk, wading at the edge of the cool water. When they got back to where they'd left the ATVs, Jillian undressed Wil and drew her down to lie on the blanket. For the rest of the afternoon they alternated between talking, teasing, and making love. Hours later, they dug out the leftovers from their lunch and made dinner of it as well.

When darkness began to descend, Wil had reluctantly packed their picnic away and they'd returned to her house to stow the ATVs before she drove Jillian home.

Wil couldn't remember the last time she'd taken an entire day off work. Even when her crew wasn't working, she was entrenched in one project or another. But today, she'd simply enjoyed being with Jillian. So much so that she could almost convince herself that Jillian didn't want to leave. Surely the passion they shared meant something. Though they hadn't discussed it, today had certainly felt like more than just sex to Wil, and unless she was completely misreading the situation, Jillian felt it too.

She was still lost in thought and driving on autopilot as she pulled to a stop next to the curb in front of Jillian's house. She got out of the truck and walked Jillian to her front door.

"Today was amazing." Jillian stepped close and looped her arms around Wil's neck.

"For me too." Wil rested her hands against the small of Jillian's back.

"Too bad you have to get up early." Cradling Wil's jaw in her hands, Jillian rose up on her toes and kissed her lightly on the mouth. Then again, deeper and lingering this time.

"Not that early." A flutter of anticipation overrode the knowledge that she likely wouldn't get much sleep if she stayed. She'd worked on little or no rest plenty of times, and this would definitely be worth it.

"Okay. Come in. But I'm tucking you in and we're going right to sleep."

"Define 'tucking me in,'" Wil teased.

Smiling, Jillian turned away to unlock the door. Over her shoulder she said, "I really did have a good time today. I wish I could have more days like that."

"You can." Wil made a split-second decision to take a chance. Their time together was close to expiring. Tomorrow she would report to the school to help her crew finish up there. Jillian would add some small touches, then on Saturday she would have her open house. Soon after that she would leave.

Jillian chuckled as she slipped her key into the lock. "Yeah, wouldn't that be nice."

"Don't go."

Jillian looked up, surprised at the intensity of Wil's softly spoken words. Wil's eyes were focused on her, and just then she wished it could be that simple. Her response faltered in the face of the raw emotion in Wil's gaze.

"I wish I could pretend to be unselfish and say I'll move to the city, but I can't leave my father or the business. So I'm asking you to stay here. With me."

Jillian understood. Wil would never be happy in Cincinnati. But it was just as ridiculous to think that she could stay in Redmond. Sure, she'd enjoyed these past weeks, but she viewed them as a vacation. She wasn't looking for a lifestyle change. So that left them exactly where they'd been—leading separate lives.

"I'm sorry, I can't."

"But you said you wanted more days like today."

"I meant, I wish I could have more carefree days in my schedule."

"Oh."

"Wil." Jillian took a step toward her, but she stumbled back. "Wait a minute, let's talk about this."

Wil's humorless laugh was more like a sarcastic snort. "Apparently there's nothing to talk about."

Wil jogged down the walk and practically vaulted into her truck. Jillian wanted to go after her, but what would she say? Perhaps she'd let things go too far today, but she hadn't thought past the seduction of the moment. She hadn't foreseen Wil asking her to stay or considered how she would respond.

She pushed open the door and walked inside. Only moments ago, she'd felt the stirrings of arousal at the thought of another night in Wil's arms. Now she stood in the empty living room wondering how it was possible that she missed Wil already. But Wil had summed it up: she couldn't leave Redmond. And Jillian simply wasn't a small-town girl.

Her life was in Cincinnati, her career, her friends. *What career? What friends? You barely make time to sustain acquaintances.* Okay, she didn't have friends, per se. There were a couple of women with whom she commiserated over work. The only thing they had in common was real estate. They had husbands and kids, whose birthday parties Jillian was never invited to. They weren't involved in each other's lives outside of work. And she didn't have a job, but she did have an offer. And she could make a phone call tomorrow and secure a position. She made up her mind right then, that's what she would do. She'd accept that job and ignore the ache in her heart until it went away.

❖

Jillian pulled a tray of chocolate-chip cookies out of the oven. She planned to set out finger foods for her open house, but she also hoped to entice potential buyers. The idea was to make the house feel like a home, and what better way than the smell of freshly baked cookies as one walked through the door. They weren't from scratch, but she had unwrapped the plastic from a preformed roll of dough and sliced them.

"Something smells good in there," Rose called through the open front door.

Jillian grinned. "Come on in."

"Nice touch," Rose said as she walked in the kitchen.

"They need to cool a bit, but then you can have a sample."

"Are you ready to sell the house?"

Jillian nodded.

"If I haven't said it, I appreciate your help with my house. I put a For Sale sign in the yard today."

"I'm not leaving just yet." Rose's words felt like good-bye and suddenly Jillian wasn't ready. "Iced tea?" She pulled a pitcher from the fridge.

"Yes, thank you."

"Sit," Jillian said, when Rose started to circle the counter to help her. She waited until Rose had settled into a chair at the dinette table in the new breakfast nook, then set a glass of tea in front of her.

"You've done a lovely job here. Mary would have approved."

"I'm glad. But I just had a few ideas. Wil did all the hard work."

"Are you going to see her before you go?"

"Probably not." She forced a casualness she didn't feel. She hadn't seen Wil since Sunday night. She had gone to Johnson and Son on Monday to settle up any remaining expenses and Wil's truck had been in the parking lot, but she wasn't inside the office and Jillian hadn't asked about her.

"I had hoped the two of you would work things out."

Stunned, Jillian stared at Rose. "You—how did you—"

"Dear, I may be old but I'm not a complete prude. Besides, it's quite clear to anyone who's paying attention that there are strong feelings between you."

"Feelings? No. I mean—it was physical—" She broke off, a hot flush staining her cheeks as she realized what she'd said.

"Was it? I guess I was wrong, then. I sensed something deeper." As usual, Rose was calm and nonjudgmental.

"Well, yes. Uh, no." Jillian took a deep breath and slowly released it. "We're from different worlds."

Rose smiled. "I always thought that was just an excuse people used when they were afraid to try."

"It's not. I'm not. Okay, I'll admit there's an attraction—a strong one." Jillian blushed again. "But it takes more than that to make a relationship work." Even to her own ears, it sounded more like a question than an assertion.

"Well, dear, I guess you know yourself best." Rose patted Jillian's hand. "Folks will be arriving soon."

"Yes." Jillian drew her focus back to her open house. That was her priority today. "I should make some coffee."

The first of the guests arrived as Jillian was finishing the coffee, and she spent the next two hours giving tours and chatting with neighbors. She was pleased to recognize several people from the diner and her daily walks through town. When she had started this project she envisioned herself swooping in, fixing the house up, and selling it, all still as an outsider. But over the past several weeks, Jillian had been drawn into the circle of residents and was no longer a stranger.

❖

"You really do wonderful work, Wilhelmina."

Hearing Rose's words from across the room, Jillian turned and saw Wil enter through the front door. Despite an intense and immediate urge to cross to Wil and wrap her arms around her, Jillian kept her distance. Throughout the afternoon she'd caught herself searching the faces for Wil's, flooded with a mixture of relief and disappointment when she didn't see her. Now here she was, only ten minutes before the open house was scheduled to be over.

Wil stepped closer to Rose, and Jillian couldn't hear her response. At least a dozen people were in the space between them, most of whom Jillian had discounted as serious buyers.

In such a small town, she'd expected curiosity, not genuine interest, to be the biggest draw for the residents. Mary had been a fixture in this town, and now her neighbors wanted to see what had become of her house.

Rose drew Wil into a group of her neighbors, obviously fawning over her. Wil shoved her hands in the front pockets of her faded jeans and her T-shirt pulled tight across her shoulders. She bent her head and stared at her scuffed work boots as Rose continued to go on about the transformation of Mary's house. Her dark hair fell forward, blocking Jillian's view of her face. But she didn't need to see it. That visage had been haunting her sleep for the past week.

Under the guise of greeting a new guest, Jillian skirted the edge of the room, moving closer until she could hear what was being said. Now Wil faced away from her and she didn't have to be so surreptitious about watching her. She let her gaze wander over Wil's back, remembering running a hand down the curve of her spine. Wil's jeans showed signs of wear at the corners of the pockets, and the shape of her wallet stood out in the left one. Heat suffused Jillian's body as she flashed on herself clutching Wil's hips and ass as she thrust against her.

"Gert, if you ever get around to building that sunroom you've been talking about for years, you should give Wil a call." Jillian smiled at Rose's obvious attempt to drum up business for Wil.

"George says we can do it this summer," the elderly woman on Rose's right, who apparently was Gert, responded. She turned to Wil. "I remember you from when you were no bigger than a weed."

Wil stiffened.

Gert looked around the room. "You've done well for yourself. You're obviously a talented young lady. I'll certainly call you when we're ready to start."

Jillian watched Wil's shoulders visibly relax.

Rose nudged Wil's arm. "Give her your card, Wil."

"Yes, ma'am." Wil's soft alto seemed to vibrate in Jillian's own chest. She imagined a half smile of amusement touched Wil's lips as she handed over a card. Two other women in their cluster asked for one as well.

Still distracted, Jillian didn't look away quickly enough when Rose glanced up, caught her eyes, and smiled. Seeing this, Wil followed her line of sight and Jillian gasped aloud as she became the subject of azure intensity. She'd never before felt as if someone could so easily see inside her. With Wil, she didn't need to hold herself back. Then a couple approached her with questions about the kitchen and Jillian was reminded of why she should. She was going home. Ignoring the voice in her head that asked her why, when she could have everything she wanted right here, Jillian led the prospective buyers into the kitchen.

Wil watched her go, trying to resist the urge to follow. Wil Johnson didn't chase women. There was either a mutual interest or there wasn't, and Jillian had made her feelings on that matter clear. Hadn't she? So had Wil imagined the yearning in Jillian's eyes just now? She didn't think so.

She shouldn't have come here. Successfully avoiding Jillian for almost a week was a feat in such a small town. Luckily, Jillian was a creature of habit, and after weeks of working with her, Wil had her schedule down. She purposely didn't work in front of the school between seven and seven fifteen while Jillian was on her morning walk. She avoided the diner at lunchtime. And she never dropped in on Rose without calling first and casually inquiring if she had any company.

Then her father had insisted she stop by to make sure Jillian hadn't discovered any problems and, he'd said, it couldn't hurt to have a company truck parked outside with all those people there. He dismissed her suggestion that he go instead. After all, she'd done all the work on the place and could better recount the transformation they'd made.

Wil had delayed as long as she could, inventing last-minute projects that needed to be done around her house. Finally, when she knew she would be subjected to only a few minutes of socializing, she headed over. During the drive, she made a plan to stay on the opposite side of the house from Jillian, thereby avoiding a scenario where she would get close enough to touch her, because she wasn't certain she could resist the urge.

As it turned out, her plan was a little more difficult to implement. Rose kept her corralled at one side of the living room, and by the time Jillian passed close by, it was too late to move. She glanced quickly to her right, assessing her chance for escape, but a couple with three kids trailing behind them headed for the door, cutting off her only possible route.

"Wil."

Her mind had to be playing tricks on her because Jillian's low caress of her name sounded like more than a greeting. She imagined she could shove those kids out of the way and be out the door before anyone could catch her. Instead, they stood in awkward silence while Wil searched for something appropriate to say.

"Hi. The house looks nice."

"Thanks to you."

"Dear, the last of the guests are leaving," Rose said.

As Jillian turned away to say good-bye, Wil sighed. *Just get through the next few minutes and then you're out of here.* When a neighbor looked at her curiously, she fixed a fake smile in place and waved. As a large group headed out the door, Wil thought she could simply fall in with them and escape unnoticed. The effort of pretending it didn't physically hurt to be in the same room with Jillian was making her short-tempered.

Jillian returned just as her face was starting to ache from the faux gesture. The room had emptied out except for one woman, who lingered in the kitchen talking to Rose.

"Are you okay?" Jillian asked.

"Yeah. Why?"

"I don't know. You just look—uh, nothing. Never mind."

"You brought back Mary's furniture," Wil said, still hoping she could escape quickly after a bit of polite conversation. But even that was difficult, with Jillian acting as if they were nothing more than casual acquaintances. Wil deliberately hardened herself. What was it they said? The best defense is a good offense.

Jillian glanced around the room, satisfied with the result. She had already contacted an auction house in Knoxville about disposing of the pieces, but decided that until then they could be put to good use this weekend. "It's amazing how a little bit of staging can make a house look like a home."

"Ever the real-estate agent, huh?"

"What?"

Wil looked disappointed and Jillian wondered why that bothered her. "I should have figured you were just concerned about your sale."

"Well, now I'm confused, Wil." Jillian put her hands on her hips, irritated by Wil's tone. "During this entire project you've accused me of spending without thinking of profit. And now you're saying just the opposite. So which is it? Do you find me foolish or opportunistic?"

Wil's expression hardened. "Maybe a little of both," she said sharply.

"Why are you here, anyway?" Wil's words stung, but it was the detachment in her eyes that drew blood. Jillian hadn't expected to see Wil again, nor had she expected that it would rattle her if she did.

"Just fulfilling a business obligation."

"Well, then consider it fulfilled," Jillian bit out before turning her back on Wil. She stalked into the kitchen, ignoring a curious look from Rose as she showed the last of the visitors out through the front. When she dared to glance back toward the living room, it was empty. Wil had apparently left as well.

Good riddance. A business obligation? What the hell did that mean? Was Jillian nothing more than business to her? She'd done the job and had her fun in the process and now was ready to wash her hands of Jillian. And why should that bother Jillian so much? After all, she'd never put it in such cold terms, but she had agreed it was temporary and physical.

CHAPTER FOURTEEN

Damn it!" Jillian flung the bedroom door shut behind her because she needed to slam something. But the loud bang did nothing to ease her irritation. Overall, the open house had been a success. One young family seemed very interested in the house, and Jillian had exchanged numbers with their agent. She should be concentrating on that instead of letting Wil get under her skin. She paced the length of the room, trying not to think about what emotions hid beneath Wil's cool exterior.

Her gaze landed on the bureau and, remembering the photo album she'd tucked in one of the drawers weeks ago, she crossed the room. She pulled open the handle a bit too hard and, distracted, she didn't catch the drawer as it flew out.

"Ow, shit," she cried. She grabbed her foot and hopped to the bed. A red line ran across the top of her foot and a knot was already forming. She stood and gingerly bore weight, and when the throbbing didn't increase she decided nothing was broken.

The drawer lay upside down and something was taped to the bottom of it. Jillian limped over and lowered herself to the floor. She slid her finger beneath the yellowed envelope and the aged adhesive came free easily. It was a letter, addressed to Aunt Mary. Jillian carefully slipped the piece of paper from the envelope and unfolded it.

Dearest Mary,

Words cannot express what you mean to me. These past years have been the happiest of my life. I love you with all my heart, and while I don't understand your choice, I respect your decision. I wish I could say that we would always be friends, but I fear I'm not strong enough to watch you make a life with him when I want you for my own. I hope you find happiness.

Yours always,
Rose

Jillian stared at the flowing script and tried to reconcile the woman she'd come to know with the heartbroken soul who wrote this letter. She knew Rose had never married and now she knew why. Had Rose met anyone else in the years since Mary? Recalling the touches of sadness she'd seen in Rose, she guessed that, if she had, none had measured up to the true love of her life.

❖

"Jillian, what a lovely surprise. Come in." Rose stepped back and waited for Jillian to enter. "I was just making some tea. Would you like some?"

"No, thank you."

Jillian followed her to the kitchen and waited while she

poured steaming water into a delicate china cup. She carried it to the table and sat down.

"Have a seat. Did you get any serious inquiries yesterday?"

"Maybe. One couple with young children showed interest. They wanted to think about it. But I'm confident they'll make an offer."

"That's good news."

Uncertain how to broach the subject except to be direct, Jillian pulled the worn envelope from her purse. Torn between curiosity and respect for Rose's privacy, Jillian had tucked the letter in a drawer until she could return it this morning. "I found this among Mary's things and thought you might want to have it."

Rose's eyes were riveted on the letter Jillian held out, but she didn't take it.

Jillian laid it on the table. "Well, I don't think I should be the one to throw it away. I'm sorry. I read it before I realized who it was from."

Rose finally picked it up and slowly, almost reverently, ran a finger over Mary's name on the outside of the envelope.

"You and Mary were more than just friends."

"It doesn't matter now."

"I think it does. You obviously cared for her very much."

Rose sighed. "It was ages ago. I was a naïve girl. When you're in your twenties you think anything is possible. But reality is a bit colder."

"Just yesterday you were trying to convince me anything was possible."

"Those were different times. We weren't supposed to be open. This town wouldn't have accepted us, and Mary couldn't live like that. I made my own attempts at conformity, but the only happiness that ever brought me was my daughter. Mary was apparently more successful than I."

Jillian recognized the sorrow in Rose's tone. "She broke your heart."

"She was ashamed of us," Rose said tersely.

The urge to defend Mary was overshadowed by the tears in Rose's eyes. Jillian couldn't imagine loving someone so much that the wound was still fresh fifty years later. *Will I still wonder what I could have had with Wil fifty years from now?*

"It's all history now. They were married for fifty-five years. I'm sure she had a happy life," Rose said, as if Mary's happiness was all that mattered.

"She kept the letter."

"Do you suppose that brings me any comfort now?"

Would it? What difference did it really make to find out that Mary probably loved Rose to her dying day? They were still robbed of a life together. And at least if Mary was happy Rose could feel it was worth it, but if they were both miserable it was a waste.

"There's nothing I can do to change it now." Rose stood and crossed the kitchen. She tucked the letter in a drawer and Jillian wondered what the steel in her spine cost her. "The question is what are *you* going to do?"

Jillian considered the question. A week ago, she'd thought she knew what direction she was heading in. "One part of me wants to get in my car and drive away as fast as I can."

"And the other part?"

Jillian sighed. "Maybe it's as you said. It's all history now."

"Is it? Walking away was the hardest thing I've ever done."

"Would you do it again?"

"No." Rose shook her head firmly. "I've learned a few

things over the years. I thought I was being selfless, giving her what she asked for, when really I was just frightened."

"Of what?"

"That I could never be enough. That if I fought for her, she would still choose him."

"Well, this isn't the same situation. There is no *him*."

"No. But the thing I didn't realize at the time was that she was just as scared as I was."

"And you think Wil is scared?"

"Sweetheart, this is a small town, and I've known Wilhelmina since she was very young." Rose reached across the table and covered Jillian's hand with hers. "And I can tell you, without a doubt, that child is petrified."

"Of what?"

"Of you."

"Me?"

Rose studied Jillian with kind, moist eyes. "She's afraid she won't be able to keep you happy. That you'll miss the city and want to leave."

Suddenly Jillian understood. "Like her mother did."

"Do you love her?"

Jillian nodded, swallowing against a sudden ache in her throat.

"Then hold on to that. There *is* a way to work everything else out."

❖

Jillian stood at the edge of the woods, where the clearing opened and stretched down to the lake. Directly in front of her sat the camo ATV devoid of its rider. Jillian searched the shoreline and found her sitting close to the water with her knees pulled up to her chest. Wil stared over the lake and

Jillian could only see her profile. Regardless, she was too far away to study her expression. The sun was only an hour from touching the horizon, then Wil would be a silhouette.

After her talk with Rose, she'd taken a walk to clear her head. She kept replaying Rose's promise that they could find a way to work everything out. But she still had her doubts. She'd never quite bought the whole love-conquers-all thing. This was real life, and there were worlds between her and Wil. Naturally, she would miss her. Their connection was stronger than any Jillian had felt before, like a physical cord strung between two hearts.

But as Wil said, she couldn't leave Redmond. So then the question became, could Jillian leave the convenience of city life behind her? In Redmond, she couldn't see the latest theater production or order Chinese takeout on a whim. Here there were no new condos to sell or high-rise development deals.

As Jillian had reached the town square, she'd paused and taken a deep breath of the freshest air she'd ever filled her lungs with. The front door of the pharmacy opened and a woman ushered two small boys onto the sidewalk. The elder couldn't be more than five years old, and as his mother reached for his hand, he sneezed. She grabbed his wrist before he would wipe his fist under his nose, then bent and pulled a tissue out of her purse. The woman was probably on a first-name basis with the pharmacist. She could call the clinic doctor in the middle of the night for a child's fever and he would probably make a house call.

Jillian had continued through the square and turned down the street toward home. By now she knew the exact spot where the sidewalk bowed and allowed a ridge of root from a large oak tree to peek through. She had pored through the contrasts between Redmond and Cincinnati until she realized she had really only one decision to make. She could compare the superficial aspects of both places, but that had nothing to do with the value she now sought. She'd never felt anything was missing from her life, until she'd come here.

Clarity came as she mounted the steps to Mary's house. After making several phone calls, she'd grabbed her keys and set out again, this time in the car. She'd made her decision, and now she owed Wil this conversation before she considered things settled between them.

But first she wanted to look at her for a moment longer. It didn't seem possible that in only six weeks, this woman had come to mean so much to her. Wil had cared for her and challenged her like no woman ever had. She had found in a contractor in Redmond, Tennessee, something she hadn't even realized she'd been searching for.

When Wil stood and turned, Jillian stepped out of the shadows and walked toward her. She was close enough to see Wil's face when she noticed Jillian's presence, and her heart sank as a door slammed between them. She stopped a few feet from Wil.

"I didn't take the offer." Jillian paused but Wil's expression remained stoic. "I'm opening my own firm instead."

"Congratulations."

"Thanks. I'm starting out small, working from home to save expenses."

"You walked all the way down here to tell me that?"

Jillian moved forward, pausing next to Wil's ATV. She touched the hand grip nervously, wishing she could read something in Wil's eyes. "I came to offer you a job."

"A job?"

"Yeah, I need some help making the changes to Mary's house—well, my house, actually—in order to create a suitable office and reception area. I was thinking about turning the dining room into an office. Then I could close the pocket doors while meeting with clients."

"Rose said you expected to get an offer on the house."

"Yes. I told them I wasn't selling but that I knew of a cute little starter house. And I gave them Rose's number."

Wil stared at her.

"Well, are you interested or not, because I'm sure there are plenty of other contractors who would jump at—" Jillian yelped when Wil swept her into her arms, then moaned softly as their lips met.

Clinging to Wil, Jillian returned her kiss with all of the emotion flooding her heart. Wil's arms tightened around Jillian's waist even as she drew back to look at her.

"You're staying?"

Jillian hoped she could someday erase the hint of fear in Wil's eyes. She nodded. "You didn't just kiss me so I would give Johnson and Son the job, did you?"

The half-smile Jillian was so fond of lifted one side of Wil's mouth. "Well, you better not be letting any other contractors near your place."

Jillian kissed her again and stroked her jaw. "I won't."

"What changed your mind?"

She touched Wil's cheek. "Mary and Rose were a couple."

Wil nodded.

"You're not surprised."

"I suspected." Wil's arms dropped away from her waist, but she caught one of Jillian's hands and led her toward the beach. "I grew up here, and years ago there were rumors."

"Why didn't you tell me?"

"Rose never confided in me personally. And I don't like gossip, especially not about someone who's been so kind to me. It wasn't my place to tell you. What does this have to do with us?"

"I wondered if Mary ever regretted her decision." They walked along the shore until they reached a large boulder, then sat down together. Jillian angled toward Wil, tucking one leg beneath her. "I don't want regrets. Rose believes Mary was ashamed of them, and it's too late to fix that. So I want to make it clear that I'm not ashamed of loving you."

"Are you sure?"

"Sure that I love you?"

"No. But you can keep saying that if you want to."

Jillian squeezed Wil's hand. "I love you."

Wil smiled. "I meant, are you sure you want to live in Redmond?"

"What are you worried about?"

"I'm never going to make a lot of money. I'll probably be driving the same work truck for the next ten years. I can't buy you fancy things."

"Are you really telling me again that you're not good enough?" Jillian stood up and paced away a step. "This has never been about money and you know that. I make my own money. Nor is it about your personal worth, because you're the only person who seems to have doubts about that."

"Since I was a kid—"

"I know. But, Wil, I've been here for weeks and I haven't heard anyone say one bad thing about you. You're honest, generous, and one of the hardest-working people in this town, and everyone knows it but you."

"I just—"

"No. This is about you and me. Nothing else." She took both of Wil's hands in hers and looked her in the eye. "Do you want to be with me?"

"More than anything."

"That's all that matters. Trust me, communicate with me. And I have it on good authority that we can work everything else out." Jillian tugged Wil off the boulder. "Now are you going to give me a ride back, or do I have to walk?"

Wil gave an exaggerated bow and swept her arm toward the ATV. "Your chariot awaits, my lady."

Jillian laughed and looped her arm around Wil's waist as they walked. "Someday I'll break you of those Southern manners."

"Now, that sounds promising." Wil's mouth spread into a wolfish grin. She pulled Jillian to a stop and kissed her thoroughly. "But they're pretty deeply ingrained, so that could take a while."

"I've got the rest of my life."

EPILOGUE

Jillian's short skirt stretched tight across her thighs as she got out of her BMW. She reached back through the window and grabbed her Calvin Klein blazer, but rather than put it on, she draped it over her arm. The midday sun had driven the mercury into an uncomfortable zone, and her silk blouse already clung to her. She couldn't wait to get inside and out of these clothes. Maybe she would change into Wil's favorite jean shorts and a white tank top, and just for Wil she would forgo a bra.

She smiled when she noticed Wil's truck in the driveway of Mary's—er, her new house. Considering it had been weeks since they had seen each other, most likely Wil would have her suit off her in minutes and she wouldn't need to worry about what to wear for some time. She'd been in Cincinnati packing her condo and making arrangements for a permanent move. Beginning today she was a resident of Redmond. Well, technically, the rest of her things wouldn't be delivered until this weekend, but she decided the two suitcases in her trunk made it official.

As she crossed the yard toward the porch, the front door opened and Wil stepped outside. Her black T-shirt was tucked into stained blue jeans that hung loosely on her hips. Wil met her at the top step and pulled her close.

"Nice skirt," Wil murmured, taking a second to admire long, black-stocking-encased legs before covering Jillian's mouth in a passionate kiss that had been building for two weeks.

"I wore it just for you," Jillian said when they both needed to breathe. "This is nice to come home to."

Wil would never tire of hearing Jillian call Redmond home. They'd talked every night in the three weeks Jillian had been gone, and she'd finally stopped worrying each time that Jillian would say she'd changed her mind.

"What have you been into?" Jillian rubbed her thumb over Wil's jaw. "Is this paint?"

Wil grinned. "I've been busy while you were gone."

"Hmm. Well, you can show me what you've done later. Right now, I need to get you out of those jeans." Jillian pulled her toward the door.

Wil's libido kicked up in response to Jillian's words and the low growl in her voice. She'd been ready the minute she saw Jillian striding across the lawn in that impossibly sexy skirt and rumpled blouse.

"This will just take a minute."

When Jillian opened the front door, Wil moved behind her and covered her eyes.

"What are you doing?"

"No peeking. I have a surprise for you."

"Don't let me trip and land on my face." Jillian shuffled forward, her arms out in preparation for a fall.

"Don't worry. I won't let anything happen to your gorgeous face." Wil guided her through the living room. As they walked, Jillian slowed and pressed back into her. Wil cleared her throat but failed to cover a moan as Jillian's ass rocked into her crotch.

"Are we almost there?" Jillian asked innocently.

"Ah, yeah. Ready? Here's your new office."

Wil removed her hands and Jillian looked around. They stood in the doorway to the dining room. Wil had painted it the same yellow Jillian had picked out that day in the hardware store. The crisp white crown molding contrasted nicely, and the overall effect was light and airy. She'd moved in one of Mary's bookcases and a large antique desk she'd found at an auction the weekend before.

"Wil, it's perfect." Jillian turned and Wil's breath caught at the radiant smile on her face. She couldn't believe this beautiful woman was in her life, but she planned to do everything she could to keep her there. "I told you it was a great color."

Wil grinned. "And you were right. It needs some accessories, but you're better with that stuff than I am."

"I have so much to do. I ordered a sign while I was in Cincinnati, a fancy one that hangs on a wrought-iron frame. Sealy Realty. What do you think?"

"It definitely has a ring to it." Wil wrapped her arms around Jillian's waist and kissed her neck just below her ear.

"Well, it's a beginning." Jillian leaned back against Wil and tilted her head to allow her better access.

"It certainly is." And for the first time, Wil believed it. She stood with Jillian at the dawn of something wonderful.

Jillian took Wil's hand. "Now, about those jeans," she said as she led Wil toward the bedroom.

Something wonderful, indeed.

About the Author

Born and raised in upstate New York, Erin Dutton now lives and works in middle Tennessee. But she makes as many treks back north as she can squeeze into a year, because her beloved nephews and nieces grow faster every time she is away. In her free time she enjoys reading, movies, and playing golf.

Her previous novels include three romances: 2008 Golden Crown Literary Awards Finalist *Sequestered Hearts*, *Fully Involved*, and *A Place to Rest*. She is also a contributor to *Erotic Interludes 5: Road Games* and *Romantic Interludes 1: Discovery* from Bold Strokes Books. Her next novel, *Point of Ignition*, is due out July 2009.

Books Available From Bold Strokes Books

Dreams of Bali by C.J. Harte. Madison Barnes worships work, power, and success, and she's never allowed anyone to interfere—that is, until she runs into Karlie Henderson Stockard. Eclipse EBook (978-1-60282-070-8)

The Limits of Justice by John Morgan Wilson. Benjamin Justice and reporter Alexandra Templeton search for a killer in a mysterious compound in the remote California desert. (978-1-60282-060-9)

Designed for Love by Erin Dutton. Jillian Sealy and Wil Johnson don't much like each other, but they do have to work together—and what they desire most is not what either of them had planned. (978-1-60282-038-8)

Calling the Dead by Ali Vali. Six months after Hurricane Katrina, NOLA Detective Sept Savoie is a cop who thinks making a relationship work is harder than catching a serial killer—but her current case may prove her wrong. (978-1-60282-037-1)

Dark Garden by Jennifer Fulton. Vienna Blake and Mason Cavender are sworn enemies—who can't resist each other. Something has to give. (978-1-60282-036-4)

Shots Fired by MJ Williamz. Kyla and Echo seem to have the perfect relationship and the perfect life until someone shoots at Kyla—and Echo is the most likely suspect. (978-1-60282-035-7)

truelesbianlove.com by Carsen Taite. Mackenzie Lewis and Dr. Jordan Wagner have very different ideas about love, but they discover that truelesbianlove is closer than a click away. Eclipse EBook (978-1-60282-069-2)

Justice at Risk by John Morgan Wilson. Benjamin Justice's blind date leads to a rare opportunity for legitimate work, but a reckless risk changes his life forever. (978-1-60282-059-3)

Run to Me by Lisa Girolami. Burned by the four-letter word called love, the only thing Beth Standish wants to do is run for—or maybe from—her life. (978-1-60282-034-0)

Split the Aces by Jove Belle. In the neon glare of Sin City, two women ride a wave of passion that threatens to consume them in a world of fast money and fast times. (978-1-60282-033-3)

Uncharted Passage by Julie Cannon. Two women on a vacation that turns deadly face down one of nature's most ruthless killers—and find themselves falling in love. (978-1-60282-032-6)

Night Call by Radclyffe. All medevac helicopter pilot Jett McNally wants to do is fly and forget about the horror and heartbreak she left behind in the Middle East, but anesthesiologist Tristan Holmes has other plans. (978-1-60282-031-9)

Lake Effect Snow by C.P. Rowlands. News correspondent Annie T. Booker and FBI Agent Sarah Moore struggle to stay one step ahead of disaster as Annie's life becomes the war zone she once reported on. Eclipse EBook (978-1-60282-068-5)

Revision of Justice by John Morgan Wilson. Murder shifts into high gear, propelling Benjamin Justice into a raging fire that consumes the Hollywood Hills, burning steadily toward the famous Hollywood Sign—and the identity of a cold-blooded killer. (978-1-60282-058-6)

I Dare You by Larkin Rose. Stripper by night, corporate raider by day, Kelsey's only looking for sex and power, until she meets a woman who stirs her heart and her body. (978-1-60282-030-2)

Truth Behind the Mask by Lesley Davis. Erith Baylor is drawn to Sentinel Pagan Osborne's quiet strength, but the secrets between them strain duty and family ties. (978-1-60282-029-6)

Cooper's Deale by KI Thompson. Two would-be lovers and a decidedly inopportune murder spell trouble for Addy Cooper, no matter which way the cards fall. (978-1-60282-028-9)

Romantic Interludes 1: Discovery ed. by Radclyffe and Stacia Seaman. An anthology of sensual, erotic contemporary love stories from the best-selling Bold Strokes authors. (978-1-60282-027-2)

A Guarded Heart by Jennifer Fulton. The last place FBI Special Agent Pat Roussel expects to find herself is assigned to an illicit private security gig baby-sitting a celebrity. (Ebook) (978-1-60282-067-8)

Saving Grace by Jennifer Fulton. Champion swimmer Dawn Beaumont, injured in a car crash she caused, flees to Moon Island, where scientist Grace Ramsay welcomes her. (Ebook) (978-1-60282-066-1)

The Sacred Shore by Jennifer Fulton. Successful tech industry survivor Merris Randall does not believe in love at first sight until she meets Olivia Pearce. (Ebook) (978-1-60282-065-4)

Passion Bay by Jennifer Fulton. Two women from different ends of the earth meet in paradise. Author's expanded edition. (Ebook) (978-1-60282-064-7)

Never Wake by Gabrielle Goldsby. After a brutal attack, Emma Webster becomes a self-sentenced prisoner inside her condo—until the world outside her window goes silent. (Ebook) (978-1-60282-063-0)

The Caretaker's Daughter by Gabrielle Goldsby. Against the backdrop of a nineteenth-century English country estate, two women struggle to find love. (Ebook) (978-1-60282-062-3)

Simple Justice by John Morgan Wilson. When a pretty-boy cokehead is murdered, former LA reporter Benjamin Justice and his reluctant new partner, Alexandra Templeton, must unveil the real killer. (978-1-60282-057-9)

Remember Tomorrow by Gabrielle Goldsby. Cees Bannigan and Arieanna Simon find that a successful relationship rests in remembering the mistakes of the past. (978-1-60282-026-5)

Put Away Wet by Susan Smith. Jocelyn "Joey" Fellows has just been savagely dumped—when she posts an online personal ad, she discovers more than just the great sex she expected. (978-1-60282-025-8)

Homecoming by Nell Stark. Sarah Storm loses everything that matters—family, future dreams, and love—will her new "straight" roommate cause Sarah to take a chance at happiness? (978-1-60282-024-1)

The Three by Meghan O'Brien. A daring, provocative exploration of love and sexuality. Two lovers, Elin and Kael, struggle to survive in a postapocalyptic world. (Ebook) (978-1-60282-056-2)

Falling Star by Gill McKnight. Solley Rayner hopes a few weeks with her family will help heal her shattered dreams, but she hasn't counted on meeting a woman who stirs her heart. (978-1-60282-023-4)

Lethal Affairs by Kim Baldwin and Xenia Alexiou. Elite operative Domino is no stranger to peril, but her investigation of journalist Hayley Ward will test more than her skills. (978-1-60282-022-7)

A Place to Rest by Erin Dutton. Sawyer Drake doesn't know what she wants from life until she meets Jori Diamantina—only trouble is, Jori doesn't seem to share her desire. (978-1-60282-021-0)

Warrior's Valor by Gun Brooke. Dwyn Izsontro and Emeron D'Artansis must put aside personal animosity and unwelcome attraction to defeat an enemy of the Protector of the Realm. (978-1-60282-020-3)

Finding Home by Georgia Beers. Take two polar-opposite women with an attraction for one another they're trying desperately to ignore, throw in a far-too-observant dog, and then sit back and enjoy the romance. (978-1-60282-019-7)

Word of Honor by Radclyffe. All Secret Service Agent Cameron Roberts and First Daughter Blair Powell want is a small intimate wedding, but the paparazzi and a domestic terrorist have other plans. (978-1-60282-018-0)

Hotel Liaison by JLee Meyer. Two women searching through a secret past discover that their brief hotel liaison is only the beginning. Will they risk their careers—and their hearts—to follow through on their desires? (978-1-60282-017-3)

Love on Location by Lisa Girolami. Hollywood film producer Kate Nyland and artist Dawn Brock discover that love doesn't always follow the script. (978-1-60282-016-6)

Edge of Darkness by Jove Belle. Investigator Diana Collins charges at life with an irreverent comment and a right hook, but even those may not protect her heart from a charming villain. (978-1-60282-015-9)

Thirteen Hours by Meghan O'Brien. Workaholic Dana Watts's life takes a sudden turn when an unexpected interruption arrives in the form of the most beautiful breasts she has ever seen—stripper Laurel Stanley's. (978-1-60282-014-2)

In Deep Waters 2 by Radclyffe and Karin Kallmaker. All bets are off when two award winning-authors deal the cards of love and passion… and every hand is a winner. (978-1-60282-013-5)

Pink by Jennifer Harris. An irrepressible heroine frolics, frets, and navigates through the "what ifs" of her life: all the unexpected turns of fortune, fame, and karma. (978-1-60282-043-2)

Deal with the Devil by Ali Vali. New Orleans crime boss Cain Casey brings her fury down on the men who threatened her family, and blood and bullets fly. (978-1-60282-012-8)

Naked Heart by Jennifer Fulton. When a sexy ex-CIA agent sets out to seduce and entrap a powerful CEO, there's more to this plan than meets the eye…or the flogger. (978-1-60282-011-1)

Heart of the Matter by KI Thompson. TV newscaster Kate Foster is Professor Ellen Webster's dream girl, but Kate doesn't know Ellen exists…until an accident changes everything. (978-1-60282-010-4)

Heartland by Julie Cannon. When political strategist Rachel Stanton and dude ranch owner Shivley McCoy collide on an empty country road, fate intervenes. (978-1-60282-009-8)

Shadow of the Knife by Jane Fletcher. Militia Rookie Ellen Mittal has no idea just how complex and dangerous her life is about to become. A Celaeno series adventure romance. (978-1-60282-008-1)

To Protect and Serve by VK Powell. Lieutenant Alex Troy is caught in the paradox of her life—to hold steadfast to her professional oath or to protect the woman she loves. (978-1-60282-007-4)

Deeper by Ronica Black. Former homicide detective Erin McKenzie and her fiancée Elizabeth Adams couldn't be happier—until the not-so-distant past comes knocking at the door. (978-1-60282-006-7)

The Lonely Hearts Club by Radclyffe. Take three friends, add two ex-lovers and several new ones, and the result is a recipe for explosive rivalries and incendiary romance. (978-1-60282-005-0)

Venus Besieged by Andrews & Austin. Teague Richfield heads for Sedona and the sensual arms of psychic astrologer Callie Rivers for a much-needed romantic reunion. (978-1-60282-004-3)

Branded Ann by Merry Shannon. Pirate Branded Ann raids a merchant vessel to obtain a treasure map and gets more than she bargained for with the widow Violet. (978-1-60282-003-6)

American Goth by JD Glass. Trapped by an unsuspected inheritance and guided only by the guardian who holds the secret to her future, Samantha Cray fights to fulfill her destiny. (978-1-60282-002-9)

Learning Curve by Rachel Spangler. Ashton Clarke is perfectly content with her life until she meets the intriguing Professor Carrie Fletcher, who isn't looking for a relationship with anyone. (978-1-60282-001-2)

Place of Exile by Rose Beecham. Sheriff's detective Jude Devine struggles with ghosts of her past and an ex-lover who still haunts her dreams. (978-1-933110-98-1)

Fully Involved by Erin Dutton. A love that has smoldered for years ignites when two women and one little boy come together in the aftermath of tragedy. (978-1-933110-99-8)

Heart 2 Heart by Julie Cannon. Suffering from a devastating personal loss, Kyle Bain meets Lane Connor, and the chance for happiness suddenly seems possible. (978-1-60282-000-5)

Queens of Tristaine by Cate Culpepper. When a deadly plague stalks the Amazons of Tristaine, two warrior lovers must return to the place of their nightmares to find a cure. (978-1-933110-97-4)

The Crown of Valencia by Catherine Friend. Ex-lovers can really mess up your life…even, as Kate discovers, if they've traveled back to the eleventh century! (978-1-933110-96-7)

Mine by Georgia Beers. What happens when you've already given your heart and love finds you again? Courtney McAllister is about to find out. (978-1-933110-95-0)

House of Clouds by KI Thompson. A sweeping saga of an impassioned romance between a Northern spy and a Southern sympathizer, set amidst the upheaval of a nation under siege. (978-1-933110-94-3)

Winds of Fortune by Radclyffe. Provincetown local Deo Camara agrees to rehab Dr. Bonita Burgoyne's historic home, but she never said anything about mending her heart. (978-1-933110-93-6)

Focus of Desire by Kim Baldwin. Isabel Sterling is surprised when she wins a photography contest, but no more than photographer Natasha Kashnikova. Their promo tour becomes a ticket to romance. (978-1-933110-92-9)

Blind Leap by Diane and Jacob Anderson-Minshall. A Golden Gate Bridge suicide becomes suspect when a filmmaker's camera shows a different story. Yoshi Yakamota and the Blind Eye Detective Agency uncover evidence that could be worth killing for. (978-1-933110-91-2)

Wall of Silence, 2nd ed. by Gabrielle Goldsby. Life takes a dangerous turn when jaded police detective Foster Everett meets Riley Medeiros, a woman who isn't afraid to discover the truth no matter the cost. (978-1-933110-90-5)

Mistress of the Runes by Andrews & Austin. Passion ignites between two women with ties to ancient secrets, contemporary mysteries, and a shared quest for the meaning of life. (978-1-933110-89-9)

Vulture's Kiss by Justine Saracen. Archeologist Valerie Foret, heir to a terrifying task, returns in a powerful desert adventure set in Egypt and Jerusalem. (978-1-933110-87-5)

Sheridan's Fate by Gun Brooke. A dynamic, erotic romance between physiotherapist Lark Mitchell and businesswoman Sheridan Ward set in the scorching hot days and humid, steamy nights of San Antonio. (978-1-933110-88-2)

Rising Storm by JLee Meyer. The sequel to *First Instinct* takes our heroines on a dangerous journey instead of the honeymoon they'd planned. (978-1-933110-86-8)

Not Single Enough by Grace Lennox. A funny, sexy modern romance about two lonely women who bond over the unexpected and fall in love along the way. (978-1-933110-85-1)

Such a Pretty Face by Gabrielle Goldsby. A sexy, sometimes humorous, sometimes biting contemporary romance that gently exposes the damage to heart and soul when we fail to look beneath the surface for what truly matters. (978-1-933110-84-4)

Second Season by Ali Vali. A romance set in New Orleans amidst betrayal, Hurricane Katrina, and the new beginnings hardship and heartbreak sometimes make possible. (978-1-933110-83-7)

Hearts Aflame by Ronica Black. A poignant, erotic romance between a hard-driving businesswoman and a solitary vet. Packed with adventure and set in the harsh beauty of the Arizona countryside. (978-1-933110-82-0)

Red Light by JD Glass. Tori forges her path as an EMT in the New York City 911 system while discovering what matters most to herself and the woman she loves. (978-1-933110-81-3)

Honor Under Siege by Radclyffe. Secret Service agent Cameron Roberts struggles to protect her lover while searching for a traitor who just may be another woman with a claim on her heart. (978-1-933110-80-6)

Sequestered Hearts by Erin Dutton. A popular artist suddenly goes into seclusion, a reluctant reporter wants to know why, and a heart locked away yearns to be set free. (978-1-933110-78-3)

Bold Strokes
BOOKS
WEBSTORE
PRINT AND EBOOKS
Romance
Mystery
Intrigue
MATINEE BOOKS
LIBERTY
EDITION
BOLD
STROKES
BOOKS
Adventure
victory
EDITIONS
ECLIPSE
Erotica
Fantasy
Sci-Fi
http://www.boldstrokesbooks.com